WARFARE AS A WHOLE

WARFARE
AS A WHOLE

Frank Kitson

faber and faber
LONDON · BOSTON

First published in 1987
by Faber and Faber Limited
3 Queen Square London WC1N 3AU
Reprinted in 1987

Photoset by Parker Typesetting Service Leicester
Printed in Great Britain by
Mackays of Chatham Ltd, Kent
All rights reserved

© *Frank Kitson, 1987*

British Library Cataloguing in Publication Data
Kitson, Frank
Warfare as a whole.
1. Great Britain, *Army*
I. Title
355.4'0941   UA649.3

ISBN 0–571–14693–7

CONTENTS

INTRODUCTION

Although the time that has elapsed since the end of the war with Germany in May 1945 is only slightly longer than that which separated Waterloo from the Crimea, the technological development of weapons and equipment that has taken place in that time, including the introduction of nuclear weapons and the use of space for military purposes, represents an even more fundamental advance in man's ability to wage war than the introduction of the stirrup and the invention of gunpowder added together. Considering this fact, the British Army would seem, on the surface at least, to be in quite good shape. But people felt the same about the army just before the Crimean War and it was only in the light of events that they discovered that there was a certain amount that needed doing in order to bring it up to date. Although great efforts have been made to keep the army up to date over the past four decades, it would not be surprising to find that the full implications of the developments that have taken place in the ways of waging war have not always been fully reflected in the way in which the army has prepared for its likely future tasks.

The purpose of this book is to show how the army's many tasks fit together in order to indicate the steps which should be taken to make it ready for war. This business is intimately bound up with many of the country's main political and financial problems and it is part and parcel of the nation's defence policy. For this reason it can only be viewed against the needs of the other organizations closely concerned with defence, notably, but not exclusively, the Royal Navy and the Royal Air Force.

1

But before any of these matters can be considered sensibly it is necessary to examine the nature of war itself. War can best be defined as the use of force in pursuit of a nation's interests, or, in the case of internal strife, in pursuit of the interests of a group within a nation. War can manifest itself in many different forms some of which are hardly even recognizable as such, but they all have to be considered when a country's defence policy is being formulated.

The much quoted Mao Tse-tung once said that 'Guerilla operations must not be considered as an independent form of warfare. They are but one step in the total war.' This idea of warfare being a whole recurs frequently in the writings of foreign exponents of the art, but has not been accepted very readily by the British who prefer to regard the different sorts of war, e.g. limited war, or general war or insurgency as being entirely separate. But unless warfare is seen as embracing all its various forms there will be a great temptation to avoid preparing for some of them altogether. Furthermore operations of a particular kind, together with the preparations needed to be ready to undertake them, frequently interfere with operations of a totally different sort, or with the preparations needed to be ready to undertake them, so the various aspects of warfare all interact on each other.

Thus, instead of thinking of the various manifestations of war as being separate, it would be more sensible to regard them as steps on the ladder of warfare as a whole, and in order to do this it might be helpful to give names to the various steps. For convenience sake the terms generally used in the Western world will be used, but anybody's terms are as good as anybody else's, providing that they are sufficiently carefully defined.

So, starting at the bottom of the ladder, comes a step called *subversion*, which can be defined as illegal measures short of the use of armed force, taken by one section of the people of a country to overthrow those governing the country at the time, or to force them to do things which they do not want to do. Subversion may involve the use of political and economic pressure, strikes, protest marches and propaganda, although this is not to suggest that such activities are always subversive: they only become so when used illegally for an unconstitutional purpose. Subversion can also include the use of small scale violence for the purpose of coercing recalcitrant members of the population into giving support.

The next step up the ladder is a state of war called *insurgency* which is what subversion becomes when armed force is used against the government on a significant scale, in addition to the methods already mentioned. Further up the ladder is a state of warfare usually known as *conventional war* or *limited war* which is held to be conflict between two or more countries limited either in terms of geography or of weapons. The top step is *all out war* which is to say war which is not limited in any way and in which all weapons are used or are liable to be used.

There is, of course, no hard and fast rule as to the number of steps which go to make up warfare as a whole: this is purely a matter of terminology. For example, some people like to describe insurgency carried out at a high operational intensity as *civil war*, whereas some like to describe limited war carried out at a very low level of intensity as *confrontation*. There are similar opportunities for inserting an extra step between the top end of limited war and all out war, to cover the period in which tactical nuclear weapons are used, but not strategic ones. As stated, people are entitled to work out their own terminology providing they define their terms carefully.

Nevertheless, it is important to distinguish between the steps or states of war on the one hand, and the various tactical methods which could be used on the other. For example, sniping is a tactical method which could be used in conjunction with any of the states of warfare, although it is possibly most relevant to limited war and insurgency. Sabotage is a tactical method which could be used in conjunction with any of the stages above subversion, whereas terrorism is an important ingredient of subversion and insurgency but is less common, although by no means unknown, at the higher levels.

Two further points are worth noticing. First, the various steps or states of warfare do not always follow each other in ascending or descending order but overlap in terms of time and place so that it is perfectly possible to have insurgency and conventional war

3

going along together. War may break out at the level of any of the steps and run up or down the ladder and then reverse its direction, a fact which is well illustrated by the events which took place in Vietnam, or in the Boer War for that matter.

Second, although the British prefer to use the security service and the police, rather than the army, to counter subversion within the United Kingdom, this does not mean that either subversion or the countering of it, is any less a manifestation of war. Subversion is a form of war and countering it, or even fostering it in a hostile foreign country may, on occasion, have to be included as part of a nation's defence policy.

In practice it is the diversity of the threat, and of the forms which it may take, that makes for one of the two main difficulties in preparing the army for war. The other is, of course, getting hold of the necessary resources, which is itself closely connected with the need to balance the capability for fighting one sort of war against another. These problems have faced this country for centuries.

Inevitably this fact has resulted in differences of opinion amongst those responsible for the defence of the country since some have always considered it more important to concentrate on countering one aspect of the threat and others on countering another. In the eighteenth and nineteenth centuries there were those who favoured a maritime strategy, that is to say one based on the development and defence of the Empire, at the expense of European rivals, as opposed to those who wanted to concentrate on a direct confrontation with those rivals in Europe. Later there was the well known split between Easterners and Westerners in the First World War. Between the wars there was a reversion to the division between those that were more concerned with the defence of the Empire than with the threat from Europe.

Even since 1945 there have been differences of opinion regarding defence priorities. As a result, during the first twenty years after the Second World War, despite the contribution which the country made to the development of NATO, the army's first priority was to preserve the peace within the Empire as best it could and at the same time to be ready to intervene at short

4

notice with a force of up to two brigades anywhere in the Middle East or Far East in accordance with the country's interests. The then large conscript army that was needed to implement this policy was easily capable of finding in addition the 55,000 men required by treaty to be maintained in Germany, but it was the needs of the overseas commitments which principally affected the way in which the army was directed and organized. In the mid-1960s the emphasis changed, conscription ceased and the commitment to NATO, and in particular to the Central Region of NATO, became the dominant influence; everything else has had to be catered for by whatever was left over from this commitment.

The reason why these clear cut divisions of opinion have always existed is that whilst most of those responsible for dealing with the country's defences have felt that it is no use frittering away limited resources in trying to counter too many possible threats, there has seldom been agreement as to which commitments should have priority.

But changes in the fundamental nature of war resulting from the development of nuclear weapons are such that it is no longer necessary, or sensible, for opinion to be split between such stark alternatives. War can no longer be used in its most concentrated form as an instrument of national policy, which means that in allocating tasks to the services there are greater opportunities for striking a balance between conflicting requirements consistent with defence realities than was formerly the case. The reasoning behind this assumption is fully developed in the book and many of the recommendations made are based on it.

In outline, the book attempts to describe how the various types of war and the country's equally various defence commitments fit together, in order to show what needs to be done to bring the army up to date. It is primarily a book of ideas based on the author's experience, rather than a detailed analysis of defence facts and figures: indeed care has been taken not to go into too much detail so as to avoid confusing the main issues and getting into difficulties with regard to security. The views are very much those of the author and cannot be regarded as representing those of any official body or indeed of any other person except by pure coincidence. The book is intended primarily for those in all walks of life whose activities or interests bear upon the vital role of preserving the security of the United Kingdom. It is therefore written as much for national and local politicians, civil servants, industrialists, journalists and other leaders of opinion as it is for members of the armed services.

The book itself is in two parts. The first attempts to predict the tasks likely to confront the army in the foreseeable future and the second outlines the steps needed to make it ready to carry them out, although in this respect it confines itself to explaining what needs to be done and does not attempt to recommend how reforms should be implemented or at what speed, since to do so would involve a book of great length. The main theme throughout is the importance of understanding how all the rungs on the ladder of Mao Tse-tung's 'total war' react upon each other, since a realization of this phenomenon is necessary, both in order to predict future trends and to decide on the measures needed to meet them. Although dealing specifically with the problems of the British Army, much of the content will naturally be found relevant to other armies particularly those of the NATO alliance.

With this as an introduction it is time to take a look at the most fundamental factor affecting warfare as a whole in today's world. This is the existence of nuclear weapons which profoundly influences the defence policies of all countries, regardless of whether they actually possess a nuclear capability or not. An understanding of the nature of this factor is an essential prelude to an examination of the tasks which the British Army may be called upon to undertake in the foreseeable future.

Part 1

LIKELY ARMY COMMITMENTS

Chapter 1

THE INFLUENCE OF
NUCLEAR WEAPONS

History indicates that the following statement of principle
usually holds good. 'No country or alliance can consider itself
adequately defended against any other country or alliance unless
it has a range of capabilities matching the range of capabilities
available to its opponents. The only exception to this is if a third
group exists which cannot afford to see the first group defeated
and which itself has the necessary range of capabilities.'

The advent of nuclear weapons has not invalidated this principle; if anything it has enhanced it. It has certainly underlined the
emphasis placed in the statement on having a range of capabilities, which at first sight might seem strange as it could be argued
that if one group of countries has the ability to blow the
opposing group off the face of the earth with nuclear weapons,
there is no point in being able to do some lesser mischief to them
on the way. But this ignores the requirement to be able to
respond to a conventional attack with conventional weapons if
the attacker has the ability to reply to a nuclear response in kind,
or if he is allied to a country with that capability. On the other
hand it could be argued that if no one dares risk using nuclear
weapons in answer to a conventional attack or as a means of
starting a war, there is no point in having them at all, but this
overlooks the fact that the thing which makes the use of nuclear
weapons unthinkable is the danger of a riposte in kind from the
victim, or from the victim's allies.

But it would be unsafe to assume that a war between two
alliances, each of which was armed with nuclear weapons, could
be fought out as an old-fashioned conventional war until one side

or the other achieved an old-fashioned victory. In practice, as one side or the other came near to defeat the temptation for it to use nuclear weapons would become greater despite the danger of a riposte. If sufficiently desperate, a country might use nuclear weapons in the hope of achieving a tactical advantage designed to restore the position on the battlefield, or in an attempt to force the winning side to the negotiating table as a prelude to ceasing hostilities altogether. But once a nuclear weapon was used, the likelihood of escalation to disaster would be that much closer.

In practice it would seem that in a war between two nuclear alliances there is little possibility of either side winning in the classic sense of the word, that is to say of breaking the will of the opposing side so that it will accept whatever terms are forced on to it. The best that can be hoped for is that if war breaks out by some miscalculation, enough time could be gained by conventional forces to enable some negotiated peace to be patched up before a nuclear exchange destroys the world as we know it. In other words the function of conventional forces is not to win wars but to gain time.

Of course this is very oversimplified. In the first place this thesis only holds good if the two sides are reasonably balanced in terms of their nuclear forces. For example, although they don't have to have the same number of weapons, they must each be able to inflict a level of damage on the other side that the other side will regard as intolerable. It is an immensely complicated business to achieve this situation because it is dependent on so many technical factors such as detection arrangements, flight times and so on and this is the context within which opportunities for multi-lateral disarmament to the benefit of both sides exist. But alliances also strive to unbalance the situation in their own favour because of the natural desire to gain the ascendancy, and because there is always the feeling that, if the situation is capable of being unbalanced, the enemy will unbalance it to their advantage unless we do so first. Complicated manoeuvring inevitably goes on all the time based on two further historical principles the first of which is that if something can be invented it will be and the second, that once something has been invented it can never be uninvented.

The other major qualification to the thesis that conventional forces exist in the nuclear age mainly for the purpose of gaining time for negotiation rather than to win wars, is that the negotiations themselves are dependent on the conventional forces managing to produce a situation on the ground that leaves good cards in the hands of their own negotiators. The fact that one side has important areas of its territory occupied by the other will inevitably prejudice its negotiating position. But despite these reservations the present position is totally different to what it was before the introduction of nuclear weapons since no military defence is possible for a country or group of countries which neither have nuclear weapons themselves nor are backed by an alliance which has them, should they be attacked by a nuclear power.

Even if two non-nuclear powers are fighting each other, the existence of nuclear weapons in the hands of the superpowers will influence the way in which the war is fought, because the superpowers will start leaning on the warring parties to stop fighting as soon as there is any danger of the conflict spreading. As a result the warring parties will develop their operations in order to be in the best negotiating position at the moment they are obliged to stop fighting and will fight with this in mind rather than with the aim of breaking their opponent's will to resist. The effect which this factor has on tactics was clearly demonstrated in the war between Israel and the Arab countries in 1973.

Another example of the influence of nuclear weapons is the increase that has taken place in the incidence of insurgency. Whilst the existence of nuclear weapons makes it too dangerous for the major powers to confront each other at all, and often prevents non-nuclear powers from fighting to a finish with conventional weapons, it is still possible for a country to pursue its interests by fostering insurgency in an enemy's country or at least by taking advantage of any discontent that may arise there. There are countless examples of this happening since the arrival of nuclear weapons on the scene.

In short, nuclear weapons have completely altered the way in which war should be thought about and practised and any country which accepts that it could be threatened by a nuclear power, or by a country backed by a nuclear power, must be allied or associated in some way, with a friendly nuclear power capable of deterring its foes.

The bedrock of a country's defence policy therefore concerns the assessment of the dangers facing it and an appreciation of what other countries it should associate with and to what extent. It may well be that a country does not itself need to possess nuclear weapons provided that it is adequately supported by friendly countries which have them, but it is unlikely to be able to do without conventional forces because they will be required for many reasons besides countering the main threat. But however capabilities are shared out in an alliance, it is the sum of the capabilities which provides the defence and each country is morally responsible for all the capabilities involved. In other words it is no use sheltering under your friend's nuclear umbrella and claiming to be morally superior for not possessing any nuclear weapons yourself.

To sum up, international crises in the modern world have to be controlled in the first place by negotiation even more strictly than before, in order to prevent them becoming armed conflict, and armed conflict, if it does break out, has to be fought for the purpose of ensuring that a negotiated settlement is reached before use of nuclear weapons produces total disaster for all those taking part and probably for the rest of the world as well.

With this as background it is now possible to look more closely at the situation facing the United Kingdom and her allies. Rightly or wrongly the majority of the population considers that the Soviet Bloc poses the main threat to this country at the moment. No other power has both the capability and the incentive to destroy what this country stands for, although from time to time some other country may have something to gain from a more limited attack. The Falkland Islands dispute was a case in point and these lesser disputes cannot be taken lightly since they often have a political or strategic bearing on the main issue.

For the last thirty years or so Britain has considered that membership of the NATO alliance affords the best chance of security. In theory, from a purely defence point of view, it might be possible to work out defence arrangements for this country outside NATO, but they would be much more expensive because, instead of sharing capabilities within the alliance, Britain would have to have a complete range herself, including of course, a considerably wider assortment of nuclear weapons. The only alternative to this would be to reach a whole series of separate agreements with NATO which would in effect involve providing support to the alliance in return for support from the alliance. In other words a complicated window-dressing exercise could be undertaken for domestic political reasons which would leave Britain with very much the same obligations as at present, but such contortions have little to do with defence and are not worth examining in this book. It is only necessary to add that the economic pressures which the other members of NATO could bring to bear, would doubtless be deployed to good effect if it looked as though Britain was contemplating action which would jeopardize the West's security.

At present, within NATO, the USA provides nearly all of the nuclear weapons, most of the conventional naval forces and a significant contribution of air and ground forces, to say nothing of a lot of the economic strength. Germany provides the most significant contribution of conventional ground forces in the key Central European area. Denmark's chief asset is her geographic position blocking the sea and air exists to the Baltic: and so on. The same sort of assessment could be made of the contribution of each of the member states of the alliance. Each country makes its contribution according to its circumstances after much negotiation with its allies.

Britain is important to the alliance geographically as a stepping stone between America and Europe, as a base for aircraft operating over Europe and the Atlantic, as a platform for American nuclear missiles, as a significant contributor of conventional ground forces in Europe, of naval forces in the Atlantic and of air forces throughout the central and northern regions. Britain also contributes a comparatively small number of strategic nuclear weapons which, although insignificant in terms of the numerical balance between the USA and Russia, is not insignificant in terms of the additional point of political control. In theory it would be perfectly possible for Britain to renegotiate her contribution within the alliance so as to contribute more of one capability and less of another providing the alliance as a whole could make good the capability withdrawn. In practice the ramifications of a major adjustment of this sort are very considerable and would have to be handled with great care over a long period, especially so far as the army is concerned, because so many of the units which are held to reinforce the alliance in war are also needed in peace for national commitments elsewhere.

In describing the tasks likely to confront the army, it will be necessary in due course to look in some detail at these national commitments. But first the way in which a major war between NATO and the Warsaw Pact might develop must be examined in order to understand the nature of the army's major commitments. This will involve looking at the defence policy of the alliance as a whole in the broadest outline.

It has already been pointed out that if the Warsaw Pact and NATO were to become involved in hostilities, the only sensible use for conventional forces would be to try and gain time for a negotiated settlement before nuclear weapons were used. On this basis the most important factor to determine is how much time is needed. The longer the time the greater the resources that must be devoted to conventional forces. It is for the political leaders of the alliance to decide how much delay their conventional forces must be capable of securing. Military men can then work out what scale and type of forces they need by relating them to the forces which the Soviet Bloc is capable of deploying.

To illustrate what is involved in deciding on the amount of time which it is sensible to buy, it is worth explaining in very broad terms what would be involved in gaining, say, one week in the Central Region of NATO and then see what would be required in order to gain a further ten days and finally to look at the implications of resisting indefinitely with conventional forces. But in this last case it is only possible to look at the pure mechanics of resistance, because as soon as one side or the other had their backs to the wall the danger of a nuclear exchange would be too great to tolerate. In other words it is hardly

14

practicable to talk about fighting for an indefinite period with conventional forces, because the dangers of nuclear escalation would increase to such an extent as the war progressed that it could not be allowed to go on indefinitely.

To gain a week in the Central Region the task would be to hold an attack by those Warsaw Pact forces stationed in Eastern Europe in peace. There is little doubt that if all the national contingents could be fully reinforced and deployed before war started, they could easily hold the first Russian wave and gain the required seven days. But each national contingent has its own problems when it comes to deployment, based on its mobilization plans and on the way in which it is deployed in peace. For example, in peace the British only keep about half the forces needed to defend their sector of the front in Germany and rely on sending the rest out when war seems likely. To station more in Germany full-time would cost too much. The same applies to the measures which the other countries involved in the defence of the Central Region would have to take if they wanted to be fully prepared. Altogether it would cost NATO a lot more money than it spends at present to make sure of seven days of effective negotiating time, and the extra money would have to be spent on ground forces and tactical air forces.

To gain a further ten days, NATO must be able not only to hold the attack launched by Warsaw Pact forces in Eastern Europe, but also to hold the follow up armies which would come from Russia. To do this NATO has got to get a lot more men into Europe, mainly from America. In addition, the endurance of the forces in Europe from the start would have to be greater than would be necessary for a seven-day war in terms of ammunition, fuel, casualty replacement and so on. In this case, although some extra resources would need to be devoted to ground forces, the biggest extra commitment would be to build up air and naval forces to the extent required to ensure the passage of the men and material from America. NATO would need to maintain command of the sea and air routes from the start of the war until the reinforcement was complete, which would not be until well after the end of a war which only lasted for two or three weeks.

15

Before going on to examine what would be necessary to keep the war going indefinitely from a purely mechanical point of view, it is worth taking stock of the sort of situation which might exist after about two weeks. By this time, if the alliance had been successful, the situation could well look like this. In one or two places there might be a Russian incursion in Central Europe of between fifty and a hundred miles, sealed off by NATO forces backed by reinforcements from America. In other places Russian probes might be being held by small NATO detachments. NATO would be scraping together divisions formed from remnants of earlier battles to launch counter-attacks in selected areas. The Russians would be trying to batter through where they were held up, or they might be preparing to open new thrusts. Although NATO governments might be congratulating themselves on having held the Russians for so long, the dangers would be appalling. If the Russians were not prepared to accept that they had failed in their gamble to dismember NATO and that they should therefore accept a ceasefire, their next push would almost certainly force NATO into a corner from whence it could only escape by the use of nuclear weapons, because even if there was still enough fuel, equipment and ammunition overall, certain specific items would be starting to run out, with a resultant danger to the cohesion of the defence. In this context, as the use of nuclear weapons would be likely to lead to a nuclear response, the 'escape' could only be towards increased disaster, although the very first use of a small nuclear weapon would not necessarily be immediately followed by an all out exchange of major ones. Indeed it could just provide the incentive for a ceasefire that conventional weapons had failed to achieve.

The next contingency to be examined is the possibility of fighting for an indefinite period with conventional weapons. Some people believe that if the Russians could be held for long enough to allow the Western nations to get a permanent lifeline working between Europe, England and America, then factories could turn out stocks and send them to the front, men could be called up and trained, and a situation similar to that which existed in previous wars might ensue. For this to happen an

16

enormous investment would be required in warlike stocks, such as ammunition, in order to keep the war going until the factories were ready to replace stocks used in combat and an even more colossal investment would be needed to increase the size of naval and air forces in order to keep a permanent lifeline open between America and Europe, a very different matter to moving one batch of reinforcements over a two-week period as described earlier. In any case, the resulting situation would have nothing in common with previous wars because the nuclear weapons would still be there with the danger of them being used increasing day by day. Nevertheless, in the context of buying more time, this option does exist, at any rate in theory, and it could be relevant to a situation where the enemy's attack was delivered at a very low operational level. But it must be understood that the investment that would be needed to make it work would be of a totally different order to anything that has been contemplated at any time since the end of the Second World War. Furthermore, the money that would have to be spent on the naval and air forces needed to keep open the Atlantic routes, would have to be in addition to the large sums that would have to be spent on NATO ground forces to enable them to hold off the Russian ground forces: the two forms of expenditure are in no way alternatives.

But this purely illustrative examination of the implications of gaining various amounts of time in which to get negotiations going before the onset of nuclear war, is greatly oversimplified for many reasons, not least because it is restricted to the Central Region of NATO. Developments in the Northern Region, i.e. in Scandinavia and Schleswig-Holstein, and in the Southern Region, i.e. all round the shores of the Mediterranean, are equally important and would also have to be taken into account when determining the amount of time to be fought for. They all interact with each other. Another important reason is that in the examples it was assumed that NATO had a common interest in the amount of time that had to be gained for negotiation, whereas in practice NATO consists of a number of separate countries each with their own ideas as to how much time should be bought by investment in conventional forces. For example, from the British point of view it might be worth buying about five days of intense war but not much more. But the British point of view is, to say the least, less important than the American one, because theirs is the finger on the main nuclear trigger and they might like to buy more than five days. The other key consideration relates to what the Germans want because they provide so much of the conventional forces in the politically vital Central Region. It is difficult to work out where the interests of Germany lie in this matter. Clearly the Germans must want to avoid a lengthy conventional war being fought over their territory, especially as it might lead to the use of the small, so called, tactical weapons in the later stages. But whatever the Germans want must carry great weight because if NATO cannot cater for their essential interests they will no longer operate through NATO and without Germany NATO would be of little use to Britain.

There is one last point relating to the influence of nuclear weapons which must be covered and this relates to the situation which would exist if the present balance between the power blocs was altered. This could come about in different ways and the consequences would depend on how it happened. For example, if the balance tilted in Russia's favour the West would have to strengthen its conventional capability very rapidly since the weakening of the bargaining position from a nuclear point of view would have to be offset by stronger conventional defence.

A different situation would arise if the nuclear balance shifted in favour of the West. Although this is unlikely to come about as a result of the Americans developing more or better weapons than the Russians, it could occur if the Americans developed a good defensive system, although it is most unlikely that they could develop one which provided complete protection for the whole of the United States, let alone her allies. A swing in favour of the West would be much less dangerous than a swing in favour of Russia because the West would be most unlikely to take advantage of it to attack Russia. Certainly they did not do so throughout the late 1940s and 1950s when the nuclear balance was greatly in their favour and when relations between America and Russia were far worse than they are today. A more likely result would be for the West, particularly the United States, to take a firmer line in opposing Russian expansionist activities outside the NATO area. This could have the effect of involving Britain in more frequent conventional or counter-insurgency operations outside Europe.

A third and very likely way in which the nuclear balance could be affected would follow the acquisition of nuclear weapons by countries that have not so far been regarded as nuclear powers. It is difficult to predict the effect which that will have on Britain's defences. It would certainly not be safe to assume the same degree of backing from America in a dispute with a non-communist nuclear power as they would give in a dispute with Russia. The best guarantee against this sort of situation is the possession of an efficient British owned nuclear deterrent, and within twenty or thirty years this will be the most important reason for possessing it. It is even possible that the present clear polarization between East and West will be breaking up before that time, in which case possession by Britain of her own nuclear deterrent may be essential in order to safeguard her own position. At the moment it is highly desirable rather than essential.

The purpose of this chapter was to show how nuclear weapons influence defence in the widest sense since that is a fundamental factor in working out what tasks are likely to confront the army in the foreseeable future. In the light of the analysis provided it can be seen that a major war between Russia and the West could only be fought to gain time for negotiation but that other sorts of war are possible at the lower levels of conflict. The Falkland Islands battles of 1982 showed that even an old-fashioned conventional war with a country whose concern was in no way related to the issues of East versus West is possible and other conventional engagements in the defence of the national interest must also be regarded as possible. In addition it is also clear that insurgency is a form of warfare that is likely to crop up in many different places, largely as a result of the nuclear balance, and the army may well become involved in countering it either in support of the civil authorities at home, or in support of a friendly power overseas. All of this is the direct result of the influence of nuclear weapons.

Each of the next four chapters will cover a particular set of contingencies in which the British Army might become involved. Taken together these will show what the army must be ready to undertake.

Chapter 2

THE CENTRAL REGION

This chapter deals with the army's contribution to the defence of the Central Region of NATO's European command. This Region constitutes the heartland of the NATO alliance and its security is literally vital to West Germany, nearly all of which is in it. Unless Germany feels that arrangements for the defence of the region are the best possible, there would be little point in her remaining part of NATO. Without Germany, NATO would be of little value to any of its other members with the possible exception of the countries of the Eastern Mediterranean who might be able to work out a defence system involving a series of bilateral agreements with the United States. But from the British point of view the Central Region is undoubtedly the heartland.

There are two army groups in the Central Region, each composed of a number of national corps. The British provide one such corps in the Northern Army Group and would, under present arrangements, be responsible at the beginning of a war for securing about forty miles of the Inner German Border, that is to say the border between East and West Germany.

It is difficult to know exactly what the strategic aim of a Russian assault on Western Europe would be. Providing that the Russians consider that the balance of power between NATO and the Warsaw Pact forces remains intact, there will be no assault, but the balance will only remain effective if the sum of one power bloc's capability in terms of conventional and nuclear forces can be seen to be strong enough to prevent the other bloc from achieving an advantage. If the Russians mount an assault on Western Europe it will be because they have detected a weakness in NATO's capability and consider that they can achieve a worthwhile advantage without risking an all out nuclear exchange with America. The strategic aim of their attack would inevitably be geared to exploiting this NATO weakness, whatever it might be, and cannot be forecast exactly in advance. However, at the level that would affect the Northern Army Group and therefore the British Corps, it can safely be assumed that the attack would be geared to securing ground which could be used for bargaining in the event of ceasefire negotiations and to destroying NATO forces in order to remove from NATO the bargaining asset which such forces would constitute, if left in being.

Should Russia launch an assault on Western Europe, the operation of NATO forces would have to be geared to the achievement of two objectives. First, to prevent enemy occupation of territory belonging to members of the alliance. Second, to do so in such a way that the countries of the alliance, including those where the fighting is taking place, are not devastated by nuclear weapons.

Over the past few years, views as to how nuclear weapons might be used on the battlefield have changed. At one time it was considered that from the start of hostilities, operations should be arranged so as to channel the enemy into nuclear killing zones where he would be contained by conventional forces for a very short time until nuclear weapons could be used to destroy him. The strength and armament of NATO forces was geared to this task rather than to the task of destroying the enemy with conventional weapons. Now, because of the change in the overall nuclear balance described in the first chapter, it is accepted that non-nuclear operations may have to be conducted over a longer period so NATO forces have to be prepared to hold ground and destroy enemy forces without recourse to nuclear weapons. Furthermore they have to do this whilst accepting the fact that they may have to initiate the use of nuclear weapons at short notice either because the situation elsewhere demands it, or because the immediate situation is becoming so critical that the security of the alliance requires it. Finally, whilst

22

conducting conventional operations, NATO forces must always be prepared for the enemy to initiate nuclear operations, including possibly the use of small tactical nuclear weapons, without warning.

This is an exacting requirement and, in order to understand the full implications from a tactical point of view, it is necessary to realize that there are two totally separate problems involved. First, there is the problem concerned with the initial use of nuclear weapons, which could only happen after authority had been given at the highest political level. This, in effect, means by the President of the United States, since all the small tactical nuclear weapons other than those held by France, are owned by America even when deployed to the contingents of other nations. Second, there is the problem of their further use should the war continue and should authority be delegated to tactical commanders. In practical terms the difference between these two situations relates to the length of time that would elapse between the formulation of the request to use a nuclear device by a tactical commander and the explosion.

The process of getting authorization for the initial use of a battlefield nuclear weapon involves consultation all the way up the military chain of command and then by the political representatives of all the separate national governments before the matter can be decided by the President. Such a process would inevitably take many hours; even a day or two. Clearly it would be impossible for nuclear weapons to be used on the basis of such a time lag in the context of a tactical battle conducted at corps or even army group level, because of the speed at which suitable targets move around on the battlefield. Initial nuclear release would therefore have to be arranged either to coincide with a period of operational stability as might occur if the enemy was building up to break through a major NATO position, or else the targets selected would have to be relatively static such as troop concentrations or communication facilities beyond the confines of the immediate battlefield. The advantage of using the first nuclear weapon against enemy troops engaged in launching a major attack against a position firm enough to hold an assault for the sort of time needed to get Presidential authority, is that

23

damage could be done to his infantry, armour and artillery in circumstances which combined maximum tactical impact with minimum escalatory risk. The disadvantage would be that a defensive position of this sort would require a high density of defenders in order to hold it for long enough, which would make it vulnerable to enemy nuclear attack or even conventional or chemical bombardment. The advantage of using the first nuclear weapon on a target beyond the immediate battlefield is that it could probably be exploded on enemy soil beyond the Inner German Border providing that there was no political embargo on doing so.

This very oversimplified discussion of the problem of the initial use of nuclear weapons gives some idea of the effect which the existence of these weapons has on battlefield tactics even if the weapons themselves are not actually used. It is in a sense a parallel to the discussion in the first chapter which described the effect which the existence of nuclear weapons has on the conduct of war as a whole, even if they are not used. With that as background it is now possible to examine in more detail the sort of operations which might develop in the Central Region of NATO where the British Corps must be prepared to fight.

So far as the Central Region is concerned, it is clear that two separate influences have combined to form the current policy, known as forward defence, and which, as the name implies, requires the enemy to be held as near to the Inner German Border as possible. In the first place, forward defence is the policy which is most consistent with the overall aim of defending NATO territory, because the least amount of country is occupied by the enemy, providing that the defence holds. This is of particular importance to West Germany, which in places has little depth from East to West: a parallel with the state of Israel is perhaps relevant in this respect. In the second place, the policy provides the best opportunity for exploiting the threat of using battlefield nuclear weapons on enemy territory. A third advantage is that by defending well forward, the enemy cannot gain the momentum or the boost to his morale which he and his allies would get were he allowed to motor unopposed for some distance through NATO territory before running into opposition.

The advantages of the forward defence system can only be realized if the defenders are able to withstand the shock of the Russian attack. This in turn depends on the nature of the ground and on the strength and tactics adopted by the defenders. In this connection it is particularly important that the forward defence concept is moulded to the circumstances and not applied rigidly for political reasons. The idea is that the defence should be conducted as far foward as is tactically possible: not further forward than is tactically possible.

Although the view is widely held that North West Germany is particularly suitable for an advance by Russian armoured columns, there are three important factors which favour the defence. The first is that there are many steep forested ranges of hills which will force the enemy to concentrate in certain areas, and although he will doubtless want to concentrate on some occasions, these defiles will at least indicate to the defenders where such concentrations are likely to take place. The second factor is that an ever increasing proportion of the countryside is being built over. Some of these built up areas cannot be by-passed and they lie across routes which the enemy must open up. They can only be cleared by infantry and, although infantry are also needed to defend them, NATO forces on the whole have a better ratio of infantry to tanks than the Warsaw Pact forces. A third factor is that no matter how much concentration the enemy may wish to achieve with his armoured forces, he will inevitably be restricted by the limited availability of suitable routes. If he tries to cram a large number of tanks down a particular route, they will merely get spread over a great distance from front to rear. Unfortunately, this restraint will not prevent him from concentrating air support and will only partially limit concentration of artillery. All the same, the headlong advance of endless columns of tanks, as sometimes visualized by commentators who base their ideas on examining relative tank strengths, is not likely to happen.

Assuming that the Russian aim would be to gain ground and destroy NATO forces opposed to them, and bearing in mind the problems of the terrain, it can be expected that the Russians

25

would attack in such a way as to combine assaults designed to pin down NATO forces and cause attrition in some areas, with concentrated thrusts designed to turn flanks and cause dislocation and paralysis in others. Such thrusts could be supported by heliborne assaults on defiles, or larger parachute operations further to the rear. It is therefore not enough for NATO forces to hold a strong position forward. They must also have the ability to retain control of the rear areas and seal off enemy thrusts that succeed in breaking through the forward position. In this task they would of course be assisted by those German national forces not directly under NATO command.

The pattern of operations which each of the corps in the two army groups must be prepared to undertake has at first sight much in common with the classical procedure for defending a wide frontier. For example the first calculation which each corps commander has to make, concerns the position of his initial main position. Although this must certainly be on a suitable piece of ground and should be as close to the border as possible in accordance with the requirements of forward defence, it should not be so close as to be in range of the bulk of the enemy artillery from east of the border. If it is, the enemy would be able to fire from fortified positions with their ammunition stacked around them and thereby start with a considerable advantage. Similarly the main position does not want to be so close to the border that enemy surface to air missiles operating from permanent sites beyond the border can interfere with friendly aircraft giving close air support to forces on the main position.

But the enemy cannot be allowed a free hand in the area between the border and the main position: for many reasons he must be engaged as soon as he violates NATO territory and every possible difficulty must be placed in the way of his advance. A proportion of the corps must therefore be earmarked for use as a covering force in exactly the same way as it would have been in the days of Napoleon. If there had been enough warning of hostilities for the corps to have been adequately reinforced and deployed, the main job of the covering force would be to cause attrition and gain early information about the strength and direction of enemy thrusts. If, however, the corps has not had time to absorb its reinforcements and deploy, the main purpose of the covering force would be to gain time. The business is complicated by virtue of the fact that each of the national contingents has a different system for reinforcing and deploying its corps. Thus even those which deployed quickly might find that their covering forces were obliged to fight for time, since the withdrawal of the various corps covering forces has to be co-ordinated across the whole front and the speed of this withdrawal must take account of the time it takes for the reinforcement and deployment of the slower corps. This factor has a bearing on the composition and preparation required by each national contingent. Clearly the sort of battle envisaged for the covering forces could only be undertaken by armoured and mechanized forces, mainly because of the proximity of the enemy's artillery at the start.

Consideration of the activities which would be taking place during a battle on the main position, show that many of the troops there need to be armoured or mechanized as well.[1] This is so that they can be capable of mounting the concentrated armoured attacks on which the whole defence depends. It is most important to understand that although the ultimate purpose of the campaign may be defensive, the means of achieving the aim often requires offensive action. No battle which consisted only of withdrawals and defensive engagements could hope to succeed and NATO forces must be prepared to advance and attack as well. They have to advance in order to move troops into the path of enemy thrusts. They have to attack in order to recover important ground that has been lost. And they have to advance and attack, probably into the flank of an enemy advance, in order to throw him off balance and destroy his formations. Such operations could be on a relatively large scale. This can best be explained by looking very briefly at the way in which a battle on a main position is arranged.[2]

The main defence area is likely to consist of a number of positions and alternative positions spread out from front to rear over a distance of many miles. Naturally this means that there cannot be anything approaching a continuous line of defences

27

because there would never be enough troops to man such a fortification. In any case, such a layout would require a degree of concentration which would be highly dangerous should the enemy initiate the use of nuclear weapons and would in addition be far too brittle. In practice places where likely enemy advance routes run up against ground suitable for defence would be strongly held, whilst less likely lines of advance would have to be covered by weaker forces capable of being reinforced by local reserves. Furthermore, in order to take account of the way in which the battle developed, in some places troops might have to move several times from one position to another before settling into the one from which they would fight. Manoeuvres of this sort naturally require armoured and mechanized forces if they are to be conducted in the face of an enemy, like the Russians, well supported by artillery and tactical aircraft.

None the less there is scope for other units, less mobile or less well protected, to carry out many important tasks. For example, there are jobs for non-mechanized infantry in denying built up areas to the enemy. There is an important role for lightly protected but highly mobile troops carried by helicopters to operate on the fringes of the main position to seize some valuable feature for example, or to seal off an enemy breakout. Other opportunities for using less well protected or less mobile troops exist immediately behind the main position. In fact, a considerable proportion of the infantry in the British Corps would fall into this category after reinforcement.

But it is important to avoid confusing these well trained and equipped units, all of whom would be operating in properly constituted brigades, backed by effective battlefield communications and full artillery support, with the little groups of reservists armed with light anti-tank weapons which certain theorists like to suppose could stop the Russians. This idea, which sounds so attractive from a political and economic point of view, would be totally impractical, if for no other reason than because the defence once laid out could not be manoeuvred around. All the enemy would need to do would be to swamp the defences in one sector thereby destroying them, and move through the gap. This could be accomplished swiftly, with relatively few casualties, by massed artillery and infantry. The unfortunate fact is that in battlefield tactics as in the top levels of defence direction, a full range of capabilities, properly co-ordinated, is needed to counter an attack by a major enemy.

Undoubtedly air power would play a major part in the outcome of a land battle in Central Europe, possibly a decisive part. The soldier on the ground requires a lot from the aircraft supporting him. First he requires a favourable air situation over him which ensures that, as far as possible, enemy aircraft are kept away. This can only be done either by destroying them on their airstrips or in aerial combat. In view of the large number of aircraft that would be available to the enemy it would be unrealistic to expect no interference from the enemy's air forces and the best that NATO air forces can expect to be able to do is to establish local air superiority for limited periods as required by the tactical plan. For the rest, ground forces will have to look after themselves, which entails providing their own air defence weapons and becoming adept at camouflage and concealment. Other important tasks for friendly aircraft include air reconnaissance and the provision of close air support.

Decisions as to how best to use whatever air effort is available would obviously depend on prevailing circumstances, and the very flexibility of air power means that it is well suited to exploiting successful aspects of the ground force plan or to warding off disaster. Of the sort of tasks that can easily be foreseen, two are worth mentioning.

The first is to provide close air support to the covering force in order to assist it in gaining time for the occupation of the main position. As mentioned earlier the covering force battle can only be fought by armoured and mechanized units because of the proximity of large quantities of enemy artillery firing from prepared positions, but at the same time NATO corps in general, and the British Corps in particular, are short of tanks compared with the Russians and cannot afford to lose too many in the early stages of the war if they are to preserve a worthwhile capability for influencing events later on. Close air support could make a valuable contribution to the covering force battle but it would involve operating aircraft in close proximity to the enemy's surface to air missile defences and would be very expensive: so much so that using them in this way could only be justified as a last resort to avoid disaster. This problem is very well understood by the Israelis who almost always have to take the risk and suffer the losses because of the time it takes them to mobilize compared to the distance which the enemy has to travel before reaching their vital ground.

The second obvious use for air power is interdiction designed to reduce the impact of the enemy's follow up forces by attacking them before they even reach the battlefield. This is a most important factor in gaining more time before having to consider the use of a nuclear weapon, and aircraft used in this way could do a lot to redress the advantage which the Russians would otherwise derive from having their reserves more readily available than those of the NATO alliance.

In terms of air defence the main problem concerns the co-ordination of the activities of air defence aircraft with the considerable number of air defence weapons held by the army. For this reason it is unlikely that any useful purpose would be served by operating friendly aircraft over the forward part of the battlefield. Indeed it would be difficult enough to organize the safe passage of aircraft conducting close air support or interdiction missions in this area. The best defence against enemy aircraft is for them not to arrive at all and this can best be achieved by attacking enemy airfields and airstrips.

From the foregoing description of the type of war which would have to be fought in the Central Region it can be seen that ideally each of the national corps that compose the two army groups should consist of well equipped divisions and brigades capable of getting to their battle positions at top speed on the outbreak of war and trained in the highly specialized skills of armoured and mechanized war. In other words if these corps are to hold an attack mounted by a sophisticated and numerically superior enemy for long enough to save the West from the horrors of a nuclear war or from subjugation by an alien and autocratic regime, they should be composed of nothing but the best regular troops stationed as near as possible to their battle positions.

Unfortunately that would cost too much and every national contingent has to deviate from the ideal for practical reasons. For example, the German, Belgian and Dutch Corps in the Northern Army Group are each composed of a mixture of a few long term regulars, a greater number of conscripts who serve on short full-time engagements, and a large number of reservists who get called up for about two weeks' training each year for a number of years after the completion of their full-time service. Naturally it would take time for these reservists to join their units following the outbreak of war and the units themselves have to travel from their peacetime locations to their wartime positions. Distances vary, with the Dutch and Belgians for the most part having further to travel than the Germans.

The British, who provide the fourth corps in the Northern Army Group, are also unable to provide the ideal contribution, that is to say a highly mobile, heavily armoured corps composed of well trained regular soldiers all stationed close to their operational areas. In practice, under half of the corps is composed of regulars stationed in Germany in peacetime. The rest would consist of reinforcements from the United Kingdom sent out on the outbreak of war in the form of a collection of regular and Territorial Army formations and units together with a considerable number of individual reservists whose job would be to bring the units up to strength and to provide battle casualty replacements. That part of the corps which is stationed in Germany in peace includes most of the divisional and brigade headquarters, together with virtually all of the armour and mechanized infantry. The part which is stationed in the United Kingdom in peace includes some of the armoured reconnaissance units, a significant proportion of the artillery and engineer units, some important logistic units, and virtually all of the non-mechanized infantry, which comprises more than half of the total number of infantry battalions in the corps.

Although some of the non-mechanized infantry battalions are carried in lightly protected wheeled vehicles they should not be confused with proper mechanized infantry carried in tracked armoured personnel carriers capable of keeping up with tanks across country. Non-mechanized infantry have serious limitations in terms of the type of jobs they can carry out in conjunction with armoured and mechanized units. In advance and in the attack there are few tasks that they can successfully undertake, and that of course includes counter-attack. In defence, once established in prepared positions, especially in woodland or in built up areas, they are very valuable, although it is difficult to extract them under fire. Recent advances in the effectiveness of infantry anti-tank weapons have greatly increased their usefulness, and the steady growth of built-up areas in North-West Germany makes their contribution ever more significant. In short, the more difficult the country for tanks, the greater the value of non-mechanized infantry.

One of the biggest problems affecting the British Corps is to relate the amount of warning likely to be received of a Russian attack to the composition of the forces left in Germany in peace. In the days when the NATO alliance had overwhelming nuclear superiority and conventional forces were only expected to channel and contain the enemy in nuclear killing zones, as described earlier, it was, broadly speaking, possible for the corps to fulfil its initial tactical commitments with units stationed permanently in Germany. The element stationed in England could be used as reinforcements to replace units rendered inoperative in battle and to do jobs which were not essential in the early stages of the operation. It all added up. But this is no longer the case, because many of the reinforcing units stationed in the United Kingdom in peace, must be ready on the main defensive position by the time that the enemy attacks, in order to free enough of the resident armoured and mechanized units to take part in the covering force action or to act as reserves capable of mounting counter-attacks.

One solution to this problem would be to station more troops in Germany in peacetime, and in fact the numbers have gone up to a small extent recently. But there is very little room for manoeuvre in this respect. The existing ceiling of around 55,000 men has evolved from the original Brussels Treaty agreement of 1948 and is undoubtedly out of date from the point of view of the current military requirement, but there would be serious implications to increasing the British Army's strength in

Germany to the necessary level. For one thing it would be expensive in terms of foreign exchange costs, and for another it would reduce the army's ability to operate in places outside the Central Region, unless its overall strength was to be increased which would itself be expensive.

The best that can be done is to keep a constant watch on operational concepts so as to update them in the light of changing circumstances such as the development of new weapons. New concepts sometimes enable adjustments to be made to the composition of that part of the corps that stays in Germany in peace. It has been possible in recent years to increase the number of armoured units in Germany at the expense of certain command and communication facilities which have been integrated with reinforcing formations in England. This is advantageous because command and communications units are easier and quicker to move at the critical moment and also because they are not so essential as the armour in the very early stages of the battle. At the same time efforts are constantly being made to improve the organization, training and equipment of the formations and units held in the United Kingdom about two-thirds of which come from the Territorial Army, that are earmarked to reinforce the corps. But at best these arrangements are palliatives. The basic problem remains that the British contribution to the Central Region, though well trained and equipped, can never fully match the role allotted to it because of the limitation to the numbers permitted in Germany in peace combined with the timing problem of reinforcement.

Fortunately this weakness, although obviously well known to the Russians, is not sufficiently marked to make them risk attacking the West in order to take advantage of it. As stated earlier, each of the national contingents has its own problems which constitute weaknesses of various sorts, but so far none of them individually, nor all of them collectively, has tempted the Russians into making an attack. None the less, the better the defence the less the temptation and with so much at stake it would be foolish not to provide as strong a defence as possible.

As things stand, the Central Region of NATO is by far the best defended part of the alliance, and because of this, and because of the high risk that any operations there would lead to nuclear escalation, it is by far the least likely place for the Russians to attack. Indeed, from a military point of view, it might be possible to deter the Russians with a slightly weaker conventional defence in this area, but the Germans, whose importance to the NATO alliance is second only to the Americans, would naturally oppose any weakening of the position, as it is their country that would be ravaged if the gamble failed. From Germany's point of view the whole purpose of NATO is to preserve their borders, and if the German people did not feel that this was being done in the best possible way they could hardly be expected to continue supporting the alliance. From a political point of view there are other options open to the Germans, but they are not as safe as membership of NATO in terms of defence. The first task of the British troops in Germany, together with the formations held in the United Kingdom to support them, is to ensure that the Germans continue to feel that NATO is the best guarantee of their freedom and independence. This is the true and vital purpose of the British Army of the Rhine, which is the name given to the British Corps together with the troops behind the corps' rear boundary who support the corps and provide the lines of communication back to the English Channel.

Notes

1   *Statement on the Defence Estimates 1986*, vol 1, p. 33, HMSO.

2   For a fuller discussion of tactical problems in the Central Region see for example:
    a. Lecture by General Chalupa recorded in *RUSI Journal*, March 1985, pp. 13–17.
    b. Lecture by General Sir Martin Farndale recorded in *RUSI Journal*, December 1985, pp. 6–9.

Chapter 3

THE NORTHERN REGION

Within the Northern Region of NATO's European Command there are three major subordinate commands, one for Northern Norway, one for Southern Norway and one for the Baltic Approaches. The Region stretches from the north of Norway to the River Elbe and therefore covers the whole of Norway and Denmark as well as the Northern State of West Germany, Schleswig-Holstein.

Although, as mentioned earlier, it is difficult to know exactly what the aim of a Russian assault on Western Europe as a whole would be, it is very clear what their strategic objectives would be in the Northern Region should they decide to make war on NATO at all. There are three main objectives, each of which merits discussion.

The north of Norway is an important area from a strategic point of view for a number of reasons. First, it is adjacent to the Kola Peninsula, a major Russian submarine base and an area in which a number of installations exist which are needed for the defence of the Soviet Union against nuclear attack. It is important for the Russians to prevent NATO naval forces from operating freely in the Norwegian Sea in relation to both of these factors and in order to do this they need to capture the airfields in North Norway so as to use them themselves. They also need the airfields in order to impede the passage of American reinforcements across the Atlantic. Thus, unless the Russians were certain that the war would be over before the American fleet could reach the Norwegian Sea, they would almost certainly attack North Norway.

There are two separate areas within the Baltic Approaches which are likely to be attacked. The first is the Zealand area of Denmark, which might be assaulted by Warsaw Pact forces in an attempt to open the exit of the Baltic for use by their shipping. In the context of a short war this would not be so important to the Russians as occupying North Norway but it certainly would afford them a useful advantage. Furthermore a successful attack on Zealand with the resultant occupation of Copenhagen would be of great significance from a political as well as an operational point of view.

The other area within the Baltic Approaches that is likely to be attacked is Schleswig-Holstein. Again there is an important operational gain to be had by the enemy as well as a political one. The operational advantage would be the capture of the NATO airfields situated along the border between Schleswig-Holstein and Denmark in the Jutland peninsula and their consequent denial to NATO forces. These airfields are important both for the prosecution of the war in the Central Region and also for the air defence of the United Kingdom. They are of sufficient importance to make it almost certain that the Warsaw Pact would include an attack in this area in their plans, even without the addition of the political advantage which the capture of Hamburg would impart.

It could be argued that the Northern Region is not so vital to the NATO alliance as the Central Region because Denmark and Norway are not so powerful as West Germany and are therefore less influential when it comes to preserving the freedom of the Western world. But although this may be true from a political point of view, from an operational standpoint the two regions are mutually dependent and must be regarded as one. It would, in fact, be perfectly possible for operations in the Central Region to collapse as a result of shortcomings in the defence of the Northern Region, either because the loss of North Norway interfered with the arrival of reinforcements from the United States, or because the loss of the airfields along the Danish border seriously affected land operations in the Central Region itself. Furthermore, when it comes to the defence of the United Kingdom, operations in the Northern Region are more immediately important than those in the Central Region because of the influence which they have on enemy air and maritime operations.

The army has a commitment to the defence of the Baltic Approaches[1] as a result of these factors, but it is of a different nature to the commitment in the Central Region because it does not involve the stationing of troops there in peacetime. In addition there is an understanding that some of the amphibious forces which are assigned to NATO's Supreme Commander for the Atlantic, could be used in the Northern Region,[2] probably in North Norway, as also might the Allied Command Europe Mobile Force. Both include a small British Army contingent.

Within the Baltic Approaches the British contribution could be used in either Schleswig-Holstein or Zealand, at the discretion of the NATO commander for the area. If it is deployed to Schleswig-Holstein it would fight as part of a joint German/ Danish/British force and if in Zealand as a part of a joint Danish/ British force. In either case the force might be augmented by other allied formations if circumstances permitted. In order to understand what would be required of the British Army it is necessary to see how the battle would be likely to develop in each case.

The Inner German Border between Schleswig-Holstein and East Germany stretches for about forty miles from the Baltic to the River Elbe, a distance comparable to that covered by the British Corps in the Central Region. The NATO force available for the defence of the area consists of a large German division, a Danish division, and the British formation known as the United Kingdom Mobile Force, if not deployed to Zealand. As in the rest of West Germany, there would also be some extra troops of the German Territorial Forces available, that is to say units or small formations composed largely of reservists who are not allotted to NATO, and whose main job is to guard the rear areas against dislocation by saboteurs, or airborne or heliborne penetration.

Although this force is neither as large nor as powerful as the British Corps covering a comparable area further south, there

37

are certain factors which might be expected to redress the balance to some extent. The first of these is the terrain, which is much less favourable to a quick assault by armoured formations than it is in the British Corps area. The border itself consists of a considerable water obstacle for much of its length and the countryside behind is wet land interspersed with large drainage ditches; this is naturally favourable to the defence and, although some armoured formations are undoubtedly needed, there is much more scope for the operation of infantry units than is the case in most of the Central Region. Another favourable factor is the existence of the Kiel Canal which provides an obstacle which would have to be crossed before the enemy could reach the airfields astride the Danish border.

On the debit side must be recorded the fact that the Baltic provides an open flank which could be exploited by Warsaw Pact amphibious forces. Another disadvantage is that the depth of the front, i.e. the distance from the border to the ultimate objectives, is considerably less than it is over most of the Central Region, Hamburg itself being perilously close to the frontier.

Subject to the constraints arising out of these considerations, the defensive battle would be likely to follow the general lines of that described for the Central Region. Although little is written about the problems of defending the area, and despite the fact that a lesser priority seems to be given to its defence, it is just as much part of West Germany as any other part of the country and the operational stakes there are just as high. Certainly the resources devoted to the defence of the area would be fully stretched, even with the addition of the United Kingdom Mobile Force, and they would be totally inadequate without it.

In Zealand the problems of defence are quite different, the threat being exclusively from an amphibious and airborne assault. As a result of this the scale of operations would of necessity be smaller than in Schleswig-Holstein, since the enemy's amphibious capability would limit the number of troops that he could deploy in the early stages, particularly in terms of armour. On the other hand the terrain is more favourable to the operation of armoured forces than it is on the mainland and the total area of coastline that has to be covered by the defence raises some difficult problems, even allowing for the fact that only parts of it would be suitable for an amphibious landing.

The main difficulty confronting the defence is once more the shortage of resources. The Danish Army is not big enough to do the job by itself, bearing in mind that one of its divisions is committed to the battle in Schleswig-Holstein. Political factors at the moment would seem to make it impossible for the Danes to enlarge their army to the necessary extent. This causes some ill feeling amongst other NATO countries who are paying proportionately more in defence terms, but it is more important to have an inadequately defended Denmark within the alliance than to have it outside: as a result of its geographic position Denmark's importance in terms of overall naval and air operations means that NATO would have to prevent it from falling into Russian hands regardless of whether it was a member of the alliance or not. Thus the successful defence of Denmark in general and Zealand in particular requires it to be reinforced from outside, and one of the possible reinforcing formations is the United Kingdom Mobile Force. But the nature of this force and the distance it has to travel to get to its position, combined with the sort of country over which it would have to fight when it arrives, means that it is less well suited to this role than it is to the defence of Schleswig-Holstein. On the other hand it is a far larger reinforcement than could be found from any other source in the same time scale.

One of the main difficulties about reinforcing either Schleswig-Holstein or Zealand from the United Kingdom is that, with no British troops stationed there in time of peace, there is no established organization in the rear areas to support the fighting units that are sent, as is the case in the Central Region where so much of the backing is already in place. Therefore if, for example, it is required to add just one brigade to the front line strength of the NATO force, which is broadly speaking what the army element of the United Kingdom Mobile Force amounts to, it is necessary to send with it a reconnaissance unit and a scale of supporting arms such as artillery, engineers and signals units together with the immediate logistic support,

39

e.g. transport, supply and repair units and the further supporting and logistic units needed to man the rear areas. Even
allowing for some support from the host country, i.e. Germany
or Denmark as applicable, this means that a lot of men are
needed to support a relatively small fighting formation and the
fact is often used to make out that the whole concept is wasteful
and not worth the resources. But this overlooks three things.
First, that the ratio is little different to that in the Central Region
where a similar proportion of supporting and logistic elements
are needed to back the fighting formations. Second, that the
supporting arms such as the artillery and engineers add to the
fighting capability of the NATO defence as a whole in addition
to supporting the British brigade. Third, and most important,
the seemingly small addition to the frontline strength in these
particular areas could easily make the difference between success
and failure, so that the force consisting of no more than about
16,000 men made up of regulars, territorials and reservists,
although small by comparison with the numbers sent to the
Central Region, could represent an invaluable strategic contribution to the overall conduct of the war.

Although the army has no direct commitment to provide a
formation to take part in operations in the north of Norway, it
does, as already mentioned, provide a contribution to the multi-
national Allied Command Europe Mobile Force (known as the
AMFL) which might be deployed into the area and also to the
joint United Kingdom and Netherlands Amphibious Force
which might also be sent there. It is therefore worth taking a
brief look at the way in which operations might develop.
　　The Russian objective would be to capture the airfields, most
of which lie inland off the coast between Tromsö and Narvik.[3]
In the extreme north there is a short stretch of the Norwegian
frontier which faces Russia, but an attack into Norway from this
direction would have to travel for a long way through Norway
across difficult terrain before reaching the target. A more prom-
ising approach from the Russian point of view would be to
attack through Finland or even the extreme north of Sweden,
providing that they were prepared to violate the neutrality of

one or both of these countries. A further alternative would be an amphibious attack up the fjords from the sea although this would probably have to be co-ordinated with airborne or heliborne attacks designed to seize and neutralize static defences along the coast and the fjords. In practice the most likely eventuality would be a combination of land and air attack, supported from the sea if circumstances permitted the Russians to use surface shipping in the face of NATO air and naval power.

The battle which would develop in this case would be totally different to anything previously considered in this book because of the difference of the terrain and climate. The roads leading into Norway are few and of poor quality and they lead through narrow passes between very steep mountains. They could be successfully defended from land assault by relatively small units operating from prepared positions, but these positions could easily be outflanked by enemy airborne or heliborne attack. At the same time such incursions could be sealed off and attacked by defending forces moved to the scene by helicopter: despite the fact that distances as the crow, or helicopter, flies are relatively short, movement by ground transport is slow because of the diversions caused by the mountains and fjords. The forces committed to this battle must, therefore, be well supported by helicopters to provide the necessary mobility and by fixed-wing aircraft to attack enemy helicopters in addition to carrying out the usual air support functions, e.g. reconnaissance, interdiction or ground attack. An alternative in some cases to movement by helicopter might be movement by amphibious shipping, but it is by no means certain that ships would be able to survive in the area in the face of enemy air attack given the effectiveness of enemy stand-off weapons.

One other factor that has to be considered is the problem of operating so far to the north. There is no reason to suppose that the Russians would start a major war in Europe in the middle of the winter even if they did consider that such a time would be most favourable for them in North Norway. From a military point of view, early spring or late summer would probably suit them better. On the other hand there might be some overwhelming political reason for having to start in the winter, or a war started in the late autumn might unexpectedly smoulder for a while before getting going properly some weeks later. For these reasons it is essential that troops committed to the area should be fully trained and equipped to fight in the conditions of an Arctic winter. This imposes a significant extra commitment on the army but one which is well worth while because of the extra flexibility it provides against the unexpected.,

In general the British contribution to the battle in North Norway is likely to be of much less importance than her contribution to events in the Baltic Approaches or in the Central Region. The outcome of the battle itself must primarily depend on a successful combination of air power, helicopters, and air defence weapons with the operation of the ground forces.

In summarizing the army's commitments in the Northern Region of NATO it is only necessary to reiterate the statement already made to the effect that although the region may not be of as much importance as the Central Region in purely political terms, from an operational point of view the two must be regarded as one. Furthermore, operationally the defence of certain parts of the Northern Region is of great direct importance to the United Kingdom.

Notes

1 *Statement on the Defence Estimates 1986*, vol 1, p 34, para 432, HMSO.

2 Ibid. See also the green inset at foot of page.

3 For a fuller treatment of Russian strategic interests and possible courses of action in the area, see the article by Tomas Ries in *International Defence Review*, July 1984.

Chapter 4

THE DEFENCE
OF THE UNITED KINGDOM

No country can support its allies unless its own population is properly protected. If this protection is neglected to the extent that the will of the people to wage war evaporates under enemy attack, the country will not be able either to defend itself or to play its part in the alliance. The country's first duty both to itself and to NATO is, therefore, to be in a position to defend its own territory.

At this point it is essential to emphasize the responsibility which the government has for taking steps to sustain the will of the population in support of a war. In addition to providing as much protection as possible the government must keep the people informed of events as they develop and explain exactly why it is necessary for them to take every risk and endure every hardship in defence of the country and the alliance. Throughout history this has been an inescapable facet of waging war: sometimes it has been easy and sometimes difficult, according to the circumstances.

In the Second World War a special Ministry of Information was established in the United Kingdom to co-ordinate activities in this direction. Since that time developments in the speed and methods by which information can be disseminated have made it more important than ever before to handle this matter efficiently. Failure in this field could jeopardize even quite minor operations abroad and would render defence of the homeland impossible. In a democracy it is beyond the power of the police and the army combined to coerce the population into supporting a war which is rejected by the majority of the population. All they can do is to ensure that relatively small minority groups do not undermine the efforts of the country as a whole. Effective handling of information by the government is the only way of ensuring that the people understand the issues clearly enough to give their support. Furthermore, as there will not be time to improvise the machinery needed to deal with the problem once war has started, plans must exist in peacetime which can be put into effect at very short notice.

The handling of information in this way is a matter for the civilian government and not for the services. On the other hand it is important that the services are capable of providing the news media with access to information about operations to the extent required by the government. Doing this is a responsibility of commanders at all levels and they must have whatever staffs and agencies they need in order to fulfil their obligations.

From the point of view of the armed services, defending the United Kingdom involves a number of overlapping activities. During the years when it was assumed that the battle in the Central Region would only last for a matter of days, there were relatively few tasks in the United Kingdom which it was absolutely essential that they should carry out. They included the despatch of UK reinforcements to the Continent in the early stages of a war and the guarding of installations directly concerned with the Central Region battle. The armed services also had to be ready to assist the civilian authorities in dealing with the aftermath of a nuclear attack should the war develop in this way. But since the idea of using nuclear weapons to make up for conventional weakness in the Central Region has become less compatible with the overall nuclear balance, and as a result the need to fight a longer conventional war has become more widely accepted, the situation has changed. In particular the need to pass large numbers of American men and supplies across the Atlantic means that the strategic importance of the British Isles has increased.

Further tasks which the armed services must now be ready to undertake include an increased requirement to defend the United Kingdom against attack from the air, a greater commitment towards keeping ports and harbours clear of mines, the provision of support to American forces in the country, some of which are based here and some of which would be in transit, and assistance in the handling of their stores. Finally the armed services must establish and maintain very close links with the civil authorities so that they are in a position to provide them with assistance, not only in the event of nuclear attack but also during the earlier stages of hostilities. These links are in any case needed to enable the services to draw support from the civilian population.

It is difficult to be precise about the forms of attack which the Russians would be likely to direct against the United Kingdom. It would seem sensible to assume that the gravest threat in the early stages of a war would be from the air because that would be the best way from the enemy's point of view of disrupting the flow of UK reinforcements to the Continent. The Russians might also use air attack in an attempt to create panic and strengthen the hand of any indigenous groups that might be trying to hinder the government in carrying out their obligations to the alliance. There is no disputing the fact that the Russians could launch a significant number of aircraft against this country, although the damage they could do would depend on their ability to penetrate NATO's air defences: the direct line of approach being via the Baltic Approaches, i.e. over NATO's Northern Region. It is also worth noticing that, although it is largely a NATO function to defend the United Kingdom from air attack, it would be a national responsibility to mitigate the effect of such enemy air attack as penetrated NATO's air defences.

But air raids would not constitute the only threat. The Russians are well aware that there are many targets suitable for attack by their Special Forces, and they have the capability to use them in the United Kingdom. Furthermore their tactical doctrine emphasizes the importance of this sort of operation. Widespread attacks by troops trained on similar lines to the British Special Air Service are therefore sure to take place.

The Russians also have an airborne and an amphibious assault capability but they would not be able to use it against the United

Kingdom in the early stages of a war in the face of NATO air and maritime forces, because of the distances involved. Later on, either airborne or amphibious forces could be used in the context of large scale raids or even of invasion, if the Russians had managed to establish themselves on the Northern European coastline and if the forces themselves had managed to survive earlier battles elsewhere. This is not a particularly likely threat to develop because under present circumstances it is improbable that a war would continue for long enough for this to happen without either a ceasefire or a nuclear exchange taking place. But it is a possibility, and whereas the threat could develop within a few weeks of the start of a war, it would take far longer than that to build up the forces that would be required to deal with it, unless proper plans for doing so existed in peace.

A threat against which the armed forces would have to be prepared to help the police, can best be described as home grown confusion. Although there is some doubt as to whether the Russians have plans to organize disaffected elements of the population into committing acts of sabotage or riot in a period of transition to war, there is little doubt that a great deal of confusion would occur unless steps were taken to avoid it. There is a possibility that politically sensitive protest leading to riots would need to be controlled. In addition there could be traffic congestion arising from civilian concern or panic, which it would stretch the powers of the police to contain.

The army's commitment for handling all these dangers can be summarized under three main headings. First, there is the defence of installations against attack by enemy special forces. Second, there is the whole business of being ready to assist the civil authorities in maintaining the cohesion of the country in the face of enemy air, or even nuclear, attack. Third, the army must be ready to oppose either a large scale raid or an invasion, should one of these relatively unlikely contingencies arise.

It is much less easy to describe how the army would be likely to operate in defence of the United Kingdom than it is to describe the battle that would take place on the Central Front of NATO. There are a number of reasons for this. First, the way in which the enemy would operate in the event of an attack across the Inner German Border is well known and the tactics of the defending forces have been worked out in detail and practised on many exercises. An analysis of the sort of jobs which the army might be called upon to do in the United Kingdom has not been carried out in the same amount of detail, nor have the relevant tactical procedures been so carefully defined or practised. Second, a war on the Continent would be almost exclusively a matter for the armed services, whereas within the United Kingdom the army would be operating largely in support of the civilian authorities and it is difficult to know exactly what the civil authorities would want. Third, following on from this, the army would have to work very closely with the police who would find themselves shouldering a heavy burden of responsibility in terms of defence for which they are neither trained nor adequately funded. Another uncertainty concerns the way in which the two would work in together, especially as there are many different police forces around the country each responsible to its own Chief Constable. Fourth, the amount of effort and resources which the army would need to devote to assisting the civilian authorities would depend greatly on the extent to which the civil authorities could look after themselves. For example, in the last war the civilian community was able to look after itself in terms of casualty handling, fire fighting, clearance of rubble and protection from chemical attack but it is difficult to know whether this would be the case in a future war. Diversion of military effort in this direction would naturally limit the army's ability to carry out its other functions.

But despite the uncertainties there are at least some indications of the way in which the army would be required to operate. For example the government has laid down how political control would be exercised under various circumstances and it has also directed that the arrangements used in peace for co-ordinating the activities of the armed forces and the civil authorities in the event of a natural disaster or serious accident, should be used as a basis for dealing with the problems of the defence of the country. This means that a number of civil regions would be established to match the existing military districts and that close liaison would operate between the civil authorities including the police Chief Constables and the general officers commanding the military districts.

Within each district available troops would be split up to handle the various tasks already mentioned, on the basis of some being tied to the guarding of installations while the rest would be held in mobile units capable of going to the assistance of the guards on the installations if necessary, or of being used to help the civil authorities, or of dealing with enemy incursions should they develop.[1] Installations belonging to the Royal Navy and the Royal Air Force would also be tied in to the system so that their guards could be reinforced by mobile army units if necessary and so that their defences could be co-ordinated with the civil police. The same general framework would serve to tie in the activities of any allied troops in the country, such as the Americans.

Of the various jobs that have to be done, the guarding of installations is the simplest. For this task infantry are required equipped with small arms, infantry support weapons and a generous scale of surveillance devices. Compared to normal combat operations the job is not particularly demanding from a tactical point of view, but a great deal of careful planning is needed and in many cases a large number of troops. For example, although a communication installation might be relatively compact and capable of being guarded by perhaps a platoon of thirty men, an airfield or a port might require ten times as many. Furthermore, the guarding of an installation like an airfield may require detachments of troops to operate well outside the perimeter in order to guard against stand-off weapons and it might even need men miles away to look after ancillary installations such as associated aerial masts or radar equipment. Thus, although the basic tactics are not difficult to teach, the actual problems to be resolved are complex and the whole business eats up troops.

From a tactical point of view the task of the mobile forces is more complicated and the composition of the units has to be different: infantry alone will not do. Mobile units whose job is to come to the rescue of those guarding installations, do not have to be capable of carrying out such intense or complicated operations as those conducted on the Continent, but they need a reconnaissance element and the ability to put down some indirect fire. They also need to be trained to a higher standard than those whose job is restricted to the guarding of a static installation.

When it comes to providing units or formations to assist the civil authorities, the method of their operation is difficult to predict because there are so many different tasks that might need doing. For example, from the very start of a war the problem of traffic control might get beyond the powers of the police, if there was panic resulting from the use of heavy bombing or the prospect of a nuclear strike on the country. In such circumstances the army might be called upon to help, or it might be called upon to carry out some other aspect of police work in order to release police officers for the task. Exactly the same situation might arise if large scale demonstrations were to take place, or indeed riots. Heavy damage as a result of enemy air action would call for a different sort of contribution from the army. Under these circumstances military engineering capability would be in demand, and also soldiers might be required to help the police control looters as they did on some occasions in the Second World War. The balance of arms required for assisting the civil authorities is naturally very different to that needed for guarding installations. In addition to a large number of infantry there is an obvious need for engineers and all forms of supporting troops such as transport, repair and medical units. There would also have to be a strong element for command and control, that is to say commanders with their headquarter staffs and signallers, to help control the situation.

The task of repelling a large scale raid by enemy airborne or amphibious forces would produce another totally different commitment. In this case nothing short of a properly balanced formation with adequate air support would be of any use, the size of which would have to be related to the size of the enemy incursion. In practice a raid of this sort would be most unlikely to take place unless it was apparent that there was a complete gap in the defences of the United Kingdom. The existence of even

49

one well balanced formation of around divisional strength would probably be sufficient to deter such an adventure.

When it comes to considering the even more unlikely contingency of invasion, the problem is really one of how it would be possible to disentangle all available forces from other tasks and assemble them into formations capable of waging full scale operations. Clearly careful planning would be an essential requisite for this purpose, but in the last resort no plan can work if there are vital gaps in the order of battle which could not be made good. For example, in none of the contingencies so far considered is there a need for main battle tanks, but some would certainly be required to repel an invasion. Tanks should therefore be included in the order of battle in the United Kingdom for this specific contingency even though they are not wanted for anything else. The only alternative is to hope that sufficient American armoured troops would be in the country at the time to fill the gap.

In terms of the military commitment overall, a faint indication of the size of the problem can be seen by comparing the strength of all three services which the government expects to have in the country after reinforcing the Continent, with the numbers held in the United Kingdom in the two wars waged against Germany earlier this century. In the First World War, despite the fact that an enemy invasion was never seriously contemplated, the numbers deployed overseas never exceeded the numbers held in the United Kingdom until the year 1917. Furthermore, this fact must be viewed against the large numbers involved, i.e. around a million and a half men deployed in France in 1916. In the Second World War, some six months before the Germans launched their attack on Belgium and Holland in May 1940, and at a time when the fall of France and a possible invasion of England seemed highly unlikely, there were nearly one million soldiers under arms in the United Kingdom as opposed to about a quarter of a million deployed on the Continent. After the evacuation of the British Expeditionary Force through Dunkirk the numbers in England naturally increased considerably. By comparison with these figures the government's present expectations[2] are for a total of over 100,000 men and women of all three services to be available for the defence of the United Kingdom after the completion of the reinforcement of the British Army of the Rhine which is itself expected nearly to treble its peacetime strength of 55,000.[3]

Clearly this represents a very different situation to that which existed at the time of the earlier wars mentioned. This is partly explained by the fact that planning for the defence of the United Kingdom has not kept up with the demands of fighting a longer war and partly because resources are in short supply overall and the priority given to the defence of the United Kingdom, as opposed to the needs of other theatres, has not allowed for as many men to be earmarked for the job as would appear to be required on the basis of past experience. In practice it may well be that the requirement is neither that indicated by past experience nor present expectation, but it is interesting to compare the two before examining the measures needed to fit the army for its task.

In considering the balance of arms needed for carrying out the home defence role the situation is equally unpromising and reflects the emphasis on guarding installations that existed when the country was preparing for a very short war. For this role infantry was virtually the only arm needed, although communications and other forms of support were required to some extent. But the change of emphasis towards a longer war, with the possibility of the army having to help handle the effects of heavy air bombardment and even of amphibious raids or invasion, means that a more complicated balance of arms and supporting services is needed. In particular a proper scale of engineer units together with reconnaissance, transport, medical, repair, communication and helicopter support elements is essential even before amphibious raids and invasion are considered. To handle them the force needs to be further enhanced by extra artillery units and it needs to be supported by air defence and ground attack aircraft.

No account of the army's commitment to the defence of the United Kingdom would be complete without some reference to the distances over which operations can be expected to take place, especially as the concept of operations described earlier is largely based on moving mobile reserves to reinforce guards on installations or to go to the assistance of the civil authorities. To get these operations into the perspective of NATO as a whole it is only necessary to mention that the distance from one end of the country to the other is equivalent to the distance between Hamburg and Florence. In other words it is considerably greater than the width of the whole of the Central Region and that is the sort of distance that any central reserve held by the Commander-in-Chief might have to travel. Reserves held by the commanders of the military districts would naturally not have so far to go, but even within districts distances can be considerable. For example one important district stretches from the north of Derbyshire to the south-east tip of Essex while another takes in the country from Land's End to the eastern boundary of Gloucestershire and Wiltshire. The biggest of them covers the whole of Scotland including the Orkneys and the Shetland Islands.

Clearly these large distances mean that a great deal of reliance has to be placed on aircraft, and particularly on helicopters, to enable the necessary movement of troops to take place. This in turn means that the Royal Air Force has to become closely involved with many aspects of the operations; not just the air defence of the country. In practice close co-operation between the services is just as important in the defence of the United Kingdom as it is in operations overseas.

Another factor which greatly influences the army's commitment to the country's defence is the question of the amount of warning time of the outbreak of hostilities that can be expected. From what has been said already, it is obvious that the standard of tactical expertise required of troops whose job it is to guard static installations need not be as high as that of the troops earmarked to act as mobile reaction forces or to reinforce the British Corps on the Continent. On the face of it, therefore, it would seem sensible to use regular units and units of the Territorial Army to do the more exacting tasks, while reserving the static guarding job for units made up of reservists. But because of the time factor it is possible that neither reservist units, nor even units of the Territorial Army for that matter, would be ready in time to defend the static installations from enemy

52

special forces should they attack before the process of mobilization is complete. The guarding of installations is therefore a
task that may well fall to units of the Regular Army, at any rate
in the first instance. But even if Regular or Territorial Army
units do have to be deployed in this way initially, it is important
that they should be replaced by less well trained troops as soon
as possible so that they can be available for use in the more
exacting roles when required.

The last point that needs to be made with regard to the army's
commitment towards defending the United Kingdom relates to
the division of responsibility which exists between itself and the
police, in peace, in war, and in particular in the dangerous few
days before hostilities commence. In considering this matter it is
worth starting by looking at the situation which now prevails in
peacetime.

Before the police force existed the civil authorities naturally
had to call upon the army for assistance whenever it was necessary to maintain the law of the country by force. The army
might, therefore, find itself involved in putting down a rebellion
such as the Jacobite uprisings of the eighteenth century, or it
might be used to assist the excisemen in dealing with smugglers,
or it might be used to handle riots resulting from food shortages
or industrial troubles, or it might even be needed to capture
armed criminals such as highwaymen. If a military commander
was asked for assistance by the magistrates who at that time
represented the civil authorities, he was bound by law to provide
it, although in practice he would try to get the approval of his
military superiors if possible.

As the police developed, they took over the job of enforcing
the law providing that this could be done without resort to the
use of firearms. From the 1920s the chief officers of police, i.e.
the Chief Constables of the various police forces, took over the
role of the magistrates as representing the civil authorities. From
that time it was their responsibility to decide whether to call for
assistance from the army. Over the years a distribution of
responsibility became accepted under which the police handled
demonstrations even if they developed into riots, regardless of
whether they resulted from political or non-political causes. The

army became involved if armed men acting as a team were needed to deal with a situation, regardless of whether that situation was brought about by politically motivated men such as terrorists or by criminals as in the celebrated Sydney Street siege. The army rather than the police was also used if labour was needed, as for example when the dockers went on strike, but under these circumstances soldiers would act unarmed, relying on the police to protect them from violence. Finally it was the army's business to deal with explosive devices regardless of whether they had been planted by terrorists or were merely left over from previous wars.

This division of labour, which was not formalized, was based on the respective capabilities of the army and the police rather than on whether a given situation was criminally or politically inspired. It did not work in the same way in Northern Ireland as it did in the rest of the United Kingdom because the police there were trained and equipped as a para-military force. In mainland Britain the system worked smoothly enough until around the beginning of the 1970s but at that time it came under strain for two main reasons. First, there were a number of very large politically inspired protest marches, which sometimes turned into riots, and the police found it hard to assemble enough men to handle them. Second, there was a considerable increase in politically inspired terrorism, some of which had spilt over from Ireland and some of which had its origins overseas.

As a result of these factors it was suggested by a number of people that a 'third force' should be raised on the lines of those employed in France and Italy. The proponents of the idea felt that it would leave the police free to counter normal criminal activity and it would prevent them from becoming tainted with the unpopularity which might arise if they were seen to be involved in suppressing popular demonstrations of political dissent. It would also ensure that a sufficient number of properly trained and equipped men were available to deal with demonstrations and riots thus reducing the risk of an inadequate number of policemen being overwhelmed on some future occasion. From the army's point of view the advantage of the idea was seen as being to preserve soldiers for their primary task of fighting a foreign enemy and to prevent them from being tainted with the unpopularity which might result from suppressing popular protest.

Unfortunately there was one major drawback to the idea, which is that the 'third force' would have had to be totally independent of both the police and the Ministry of Defence if the odium of suppressing political protest was to be kept from the police and the army, and to do this would have involved heavy and expensive overheads. Furthermore, to achieve its aim, the third force would have had to be strong enough to handle a number of situations in different parts of the country at the same time, which would mean that a lot of men would need to be recruited, equipped, trained and paid, on the off chance that they might be used from time to time.

In the event, what has happened is that the police have developed their capabilities in a manner that was not foreseen at that time. First, they have worked out a system under which officers from many different forces can rapidly reinforce a threatened area, thus providing a Chief Constable with enough men to handle large scale riots. Second, they have increased the number of officers capable of using firearms and have greatly improved their ability to operate as teams so that they do not need to ask for assistance from the army when dealing with small groups of armed criminals or terrorists. Third, they are developing a capability to deal with explosive devices for the same reason. In short, the police are now capable of doing most of the tasks which the proposed third force was designed to do and which the army would have done in years gone by. They have therefore greatly increased their ability to act in support of the government in both peace and war, although in doing so they may have started an evolutionary process which could have constitutional implications in terms of civil liberties. Of all these measures the ability to reinforce across police force boundaries has done most to increase the effectiveness of the force.

These developments are advantageous to the politicians because they enable them to get the police to deal with politically inspired unrest as if it were criminal activity: from a presentational point of view this would be more difficult to do if the

55

army or a third force had to be called in. These developments are also advantageous to the army to the extent that increasing the power of the police means that less military resources in terms of manpower, training and equipment need to be diverted away from preparing for the more intensive forms of warfare.

But there are some other important implications as well, the most important of which is that the police are becoming increasingly responsible for countering subversion and the lower levels of insurgency as defined in the Introduction. Although subversion and insurgency both involve breaches of the law which the police exist to uphold, their true relevance is in the context of defence. In other words the police are taking on a larger share of the country's defence effort than they have done in the past, which even includes playing an important part in plans designed to defend installations from attacks by enemy Special Forces. Although there is nothing intrinsically wrong with this from a defence point of view, it can only work if there is general acceptance of the fact that a significant part of their task is now related to defence as opposed to maintaining the law. It follows from this that they should be partly funded from money allocated for defence since they cannot be expected to carry out their defence obligations, especially in terms of defence exercises such as the one described in the 1986 Defence Estimates,[4] with money provided by ratepayers for a different purpose. If this point is not properly understood and the necessary adjustments made, an essential area of defence preparation will go by default.

In practical terms there are many other difficulties to be overcome, the most important of which is the problem of co-ordinating the defence responsibilities of around forty separate autonomous police forces, each of which is individually responsible to its own Chief Constable for upholding the law and none of which has any official responsibility for defence other than in the context of law beaking. The existing powers of the Home Office are not sufficient to ensure that this co-ordination takes place because although the Home Office can give guidance to Chief Constables it cannot give them orders: an added complication is that Chief Constables themselves, although responsible in their own persons for upholding the law, are dependent on local civilian police authorities for the provision of resources and are responsible to them for the way in which those resources are used. Other difficulties include the fact that police forces have not in the past had to consider selecting their recruits for their ability to carry out relatively complicated military operations, and indeed it is probably true to say that the man who is well suited to the operational function is often less suited to normal police work. In any case it will take some years before a comparable level of expertise can be achieved in the operational sphere to that which is now provided by the army, even if the will exists in each of the many police forces for developing it.

There can be no doubt that the increased capability of the police is a prime reason why the government has been able to maintain its authority in the last few years in the face of industrial disputes, CND activity and the threat from international terrorists without increasing the number of troops in the country over and above the level that is needed for other reasons. Had the police not had the extra capability, it is difficult to see how the army could have avoided being more directly involved than it has been, and that despite the fact that none of the situations that have arisen, outside Northern Ireland, warrant the description of either subversion or insurgency. Within Northern Ireland, which is of course fully part of the United Kingdom, the army has been continuously involved in counter-insurgency operations for the past sixteen years, and although the Royal Ulster Constabulary is far ahead of any police force in mainland Britain in terms of the use of firearms and counter-insurgency techniques, it has not yet been able to dispense with assistance from the army. Even in peacetime it is still necessary that the army should be prepared to carry out counter-insurgency operations within the United Kingdom.

But the fact that outside Northern Ireland the police have so far been able to hold the ring in peacetime should not be taken as an indication that they would necessarily be able to do so in a period of acute tension as might exist if war was imminent. At such a moment if gatherings and marches by minority groups proliferated and developed into riots in which sticks and stones were supplemented by petrol bombs or worse, and if at the same time the police were being swamped by traffic problems, a more difficult situation would arise in which the police themselves would have to call for assistance from the army. Under these circumstances the government would have to direct the army to become involved in a number of the jobs which the police now do and the army must be prepared for this both in terms of numbers and training. If there are insufficient troops available, the government of the day might be forced into diverting units and formations designed to reinforce NATO and the most likely time for this to happen would be at the most awkward moment from an operational point of view, i.e. at the very start of the war. But the need to maintain the cohesion of the country would leave the government with no alternative.

Once hostilities commenced any protest that there might have been beforehand would probably die down and the army would then be able to get on with the business of dealing with attacks by enemy special forces and helping the civil community in areas devastated by conventional or chemical air attack. Assistance of this sort would be even more essential if the country was subjected to even the lightest of nuclear attacks.

It is difficult to summarize the army's commitments towards the defence of the United Kingdom because there are so many different ways in which it might be employed. So far as peacetime is concerned, there is no doubt that the immense increase in the capability of the police has at least raised the threshold so far as army involvement is concerned, although the requirement for soldiers to intervene in support of the police remains, particularly in Northern Ireland. In wartime it is reasonably certain that the task of guarding installations, which is the commitment that has received the most attention in terms of both planning and training, will be the least difficult to cope with and probably one of the least important after the first few days of war.

Two other wartime commitments overlap, assistance to the police in controlling the civil community and assistance to the community itself in the face of aerial bombardment: they overlap because one of the main ways in which the army might assist the community in the face of devastation would be to help bring order out of chaos by controlling looters and those in desperate need of food and shelter. The difficulty of assessing the army's commitment in these fields is partly one of working out the scale of the problem overall and partly of determining how big a contribution can be provided by the police and other civilian agencies such as the Fire Service, the medical services and so on. The only thing that can be said with certainty is that, however optimistic these people are of being able to cope before a war starts, they will almost certainly need a considerable amount of help when the time comes, particularly in the field of command, control and communications.

The last main commitment for the army is to be ready to repel assaults made by enemy airborne and amphibious troops, which is not likely to pose a problem unless the war lasts rather longer than is now thought to be likely. But this could easily come about and, although the country's first line of defence would in this case be manned by the Royal Air Force and the Royal Navy, the army cannot afford to ignore the fact that the threat could develop quicker than the capability for countering it, unless the necessary arrangements had been made in advance.

Notes

1 *Statement on the Defence Estimates 1986*, vol 1, HMSO; brown inset headed Brave Defender, pp 31–2 gives a more detailed description of the operational concept.

2 Ibid p 29, para 414.

3 Ibid p 32, para 422.

4 Brave Defender: see note 1.

Chapter 5

ACTIVITIES OUTSIDE
THE NATO AREA

Although the defence policy of the United Kingdom is firmly based on the NATO alliance, the army has a clear commitment to be ready to take part in activities outside the NATO area in pursuit of the national interest, should the government deem it desirable. In general, activities outside the NATO area can be classified as those which would be conducted with the agreement of the government of the country in which they were taking place and those which would not.

Amongst the former would come defence of British territory, as in the Falklands war, or assistance to a friendly government in opposing an outside enemy or in helping to counter insurgency. Other activities in this category might include evacuating United Kingdom or friendly nationals wishing to leave a country because of some impending or actual disaster, or inserting a peace-keeping force to assist in settling a dispute between the government and a rebellious faction within the country or even between two countries if both wished it. Yet another possible activity might be the provision of training teams to reinforce the stability of the country concerned or the provision of command or technical support to the country's army.

Operations in countries whose governments are not in favour of them taking place, might again include the evacuation of British or friendly nationals. But they could also involve a straightforward attack to preserve British interests, as in Egypt in 1956. They could also include assistance to insurgents in a country where this was in the British interest.

From the above, it can be seen that the army may be required to carry out a wide variety of tasks under an even wider variety of circumstances, some of which are far more likely to happen than others. In practice it is not worth preparing to undertake every single operation that might come within the definition of the national interest, because in some cases it would be impossible to do so in terms of the resources which could reasonably be made available and because in others the likelihood of the contingencies arising is too remote. The most practicable approach is to work out which of the commitments can be managed with forces held for essential NATO or home defence tasks and then to see what more is needed to ensure that other likely or important commitments can be handled, bearing in mind that the most likely situation to arise is one that has neither been foreseen nor planned for. It is also worth remembering that many of the operations that might arise outside the NATO area, would require the involvement of the Royal Navy or the Royal Air Force and it is wasteful to prepare the army to undertake a commitment that could not possibly take place because of a limitation in the capabilities of either of these services, unless of course it could be made good by an ally.

It is beyond the scope of this book to carry out a detailed analysis of the world situation in order to identify every circumstance that might require the involvement of the British Army, but some attempt must be made to describe the sort of tasks that the army might be asked to undertake in order to establish what must be done to prepare it. A variety of situations that might face the army outside NATO are examined here, but they cannot be regarded in the same way as the army's commitments to the two NATO regions, or to the defence of the United Kingdom because they do not refer to precisely forecast situations. Before looking at them it is worth once more considering the underlying factor that would govern the employment of forces as a whole in this field.

As with NATO, the starting point must be the influence of nuclear weapons combined with the effectiveness of the conventional forces at the disposal of the nuclear powers and their allies. At the moment two main considerations are paramount in this respect. First, that the present balance between America and Russia is such that neither is likely to resort to war in Europe in order to further their interests, although both are prepared to use their military influence outside Europe to defend their political or strategic position providing that such activity does not bring them into direct contact with each other. Second, that although the only nuclear confrontation that matters at present is that between America and Russia, a different one could become significant within the operating lifetime of equipment which is being developed now, or which should be under development now, if it is to be ready to meet the operational requirements that would arise from such a realignment.

Thus, whilst the present nuclear balance remains in existence, the United Kingdom is only likely to use its forces overseas in support of its own direct interests or in assisting American forces where they are acting to promote a common interest. Even if a circumstance arose in which the United Kingdom was not keen to become involved with America in this way, it might have to do so because of the pressure that America can exert as a result of its economic dominance, not least in the field of defence resources. But whilst the nuclear alignment remains as it is, this ability of America to exert pressure hardly matters, because the interests of the two countries are so closely tied together.

If the alignment were to change, it might be to the advantage of the United Kingdom to be less dependent on the United States and more dependent on a Europe which would in any case have to be considerably stronger than it is now. The possibility of a breakdown of the current confrontation between Russia and America in the long term is one of the factors providing an impetus for closer collaboration in defence terms within the European Economic Community, the other being the improbable notion that in an emergency the Americans might not be prepared to initiate a nuclear exchange with Russia in order to save the European members of NATO.

One other matter with regard to the nuclear balance is worth mentioning when examining the army's commitments outside the NATO area, and this is that the balance is not likely to change suddenly: if it changes, it will do so gradually over a

62

period of years. It is therefore sensible to work out what preparations for overseas operations are needed on the basis of the
present situation, whilst bearing in mind the possibility that the
commitments might be both more extensive and of greater
importance in years to come.

The first of these situations to be considered relates to the
evacuation of British and friendly nationals from a country
where the government is prepared to co-operate in the evacuation. In this case the requirement would be for a British contingent to establish itself at one or more ports or airfields and
then perhaps help the forces of the local government to collect
and escort the people concerned to the places of exit. This might
be a very simple operation, but the very fact that British troops
were needed at all would mean that there was a considerable
degree of disturbance, otherwise the British citizens would be
able to make their own way to a port or airfield and leave in the
normal way. In particular it would mean that the country's
security forces were too fully occupied to carry out their obligations for the maintenance of order and an important consideration from the British point of view would be to ensure that the
force sent was large enough to defend itself should the position
deteriorate during the time it was in the country.

Naturally there are many factors that would have to be considered when deciding on the composition of the force. For
example, much would depend on the size of the country, the
number and distribution of the British nationals to be evacuated,
the nature of the threat to them, the methods of getting round
the country, the climatic conditions, etc. The aim would be to
avoid fighting, and certainly any fighting that there was would
be limited to self-defence and the protection of those being
evacuated. In consequence it is unlikely that there would be a
need for armour or artillery or even for major logistic support.
In practice the job would be one for infantry, signals, transport
and engineers with limited repair and maintenance backing and
possibly for some helicopters if it were possible to get them
there. It is in a situation of this sort that parachute troops can
sometimes be of great value in, for example, securing an airfield

or reaching a remote group of people rapidly. In most of the situations that are likely to crop up the job would probably be done by a force of between battalion and brigade strength and could be expected to take no more than a few days. It would almost certainly be dependent on the Royal Air Force or the Royal Navy or both for its transport to and from the country.

The next situation to be examined is one in which the United Kingdom is asked to provide assistance to a friendly government in quelling an insurrection. The British government would only be able to respond to such a request if it felt that it could make an effective contribution with a comparatively small force, but there are some places in the world where this might still be possible. In any case the size, composition and employment of a force deployed for this purpose would be very different to that considered in the first example.

The job of countering insurgents anywhere is a difficult business, but doubly so if it has to be done in someone else's country because of the problems of tying in the activities of those sent with those of the local army and police and ensuring that all parties are complementing the work which the government of the country should be doing in other directions. In order to see what is involved it is necessary to see how a counter-insurgency campaign should be put together.

Broadly speaking there are two parts to any campaign of insurgency. First there is the action which the insurgents take to influence people into supporting them and second there is the action which they and their supporters take against the government. Both parts go along together, overlap and are not easily distinguishable to the outside world. In both areas the methods which the insurgents use are bound to depend on the prevailing circumstances but are likely to consist of a mixture of persuasion and coercion. Success depends on getting the correct balance between violence on the one hand and political, psychological and economic pressures on the other. In order to execute such a co-ordinated programme, insurgents have to have an organization which they can get either by infiltrating one that already exists or by setting up a new one.

The aim of the government when trying to counter such a campaign is to regain and retain the allegiance of its people. Its methods for doing this must also depend on the circumstances, for example the terrain, the sort of society that exists, and the degree of support which the insurgents are getting from outside the country, if any. Like the insurgents, the government has to combine political, psychological and economic pressures with the operations of the security forces. It cannot be said too often that countering insurgency involves a wide range of government activity and operations by the security forces only help matters if they are conducted within an overall framework that ties the whole programme together. Help from an ally must equally be tied into this framework, which should consist of four separate parts.

First, there must be some co-ordinating machinery to ensure that the various aspects of the campaign can be tied together in such a way that methods of one sort do not interfere with methods of another sort and it is most important that this co-ordination is effective at every level. It is by no means easy to set up adequate co-ordinating machinery because, even if an effective system can be devised, it can only be made to work if people are prepared to pay the price for it, which usually has to be paid in political, personal and economic terms.

The second part of the frame consists of the action needed to persuade the people to reject the unconstitutional activities of the insurgents. For this to happen all those concerned with planning and executing any part of the government's programme must constantly bear in mind the effects which their plans and actions are likely to have on public opinion. In addition an information service capable of monitoring enemy propaganda and preparing and disseminating material to counter it and of getting across the government's views must be set up. Again although it is not difficult to devise such a system, there is a price to be paid for setting it up, particularly in political terms.

The third part of the frame is to establish a strong intelligence organization in order to provide the government with the information it needs to work out policy and to provide the security forces with the information that they need to conduct operations.

The difficulty is that in normal times the requirement is best met by a small, secure and highly centralized system working direct to the top level of government, whereas when an insurgency organization has been built up, a larger, decentralized system capable of providing background information to commanders at every level is needed. Once again there is a political price for doing this because, in effect, the dissemination of information results in the dissemination of power also. Furthermore, there is a considerable security risk inherent in enlarging the intelligence organization in this way.

The last part of the frame involves establishing an effective legal system. For this to happen it is first necessary to discover exactly what the legal position is, e.g. what are the legal powers of the police and the military. Next, the government must decide what changes should be made to the law to ensure that the security forces are able to take the necessary action without breaking it. In addition the way in which the law is administered may have to be altered to take account of the vulnerability to intimidation of judges, juries and prosecutors.

One last point regarding the framework is that each part of it depends to some extent on the other parts and has to be changed as the campaign develops to take account of changing circumstances. The business of building up and manipulating the framework is one of the most complicated aspects of defeating insurgents.

Once plans are in train for the establishment of a workable framework it is time to start thinking about the operations of the security forces. First, there are defensive operations, which are those designed to prevent the insurgents from achieving their aims. Second are offensive operations designed to root out the insurgents themselves. Politicians normally favour defensive operations because they are sensitive to enemy successes and to the propaganda aimed at them if they use their security forces offensively. Certainly if too little emphasis is placed upon defensive operations the enemy is able to get cheap success which enhances his reputation. At the same time if too little emphasis is placed on offensive operations, the insurgent organization is able to expand easily which means that more and more resources have to be expended by the government on defensive tasks, merely to maintain its position.

The sort of tasks which fall under the heading of defensive operations include the guarding of factories, docks, commercial centres, security force bases and people who are at particular risk, such as politicians and judges. Defensive operations also include the protection of legal marches and rallies and the dispersal of illegal ones and riots. In rural areas they could also include the protection of crops. Taking the business one stage further, defensive operations can also include the forging of links with the population, often described as community relations, and even methods of population control fall under this heading. The common factor in all these different operations is that they are designed to prevent the enemy from doing something.

Offensive action which is aimed at identifying and destroying the insurgents, is mainly concerned with obtaining information and deploying resources to take advantage of it. In order to do this a tactical commander at any level has to use his forces to build up a picture by patrolling and observing. He can then add information discovered in this way to that provided by the intelligence organization and use it for offensive purposes when he has enough to make success probable. If he takes offensive action without adequate information he will not only fail in his aim but will in all probability cause unnecessary annoyance to the population, thereby risking a loss of support to the government. Special forces, i.e. those that are equipped, trained or recruited to carry out a special role, are often particularly suitable for carrying out offensive operations but their activities must be fully co-ordinated with other security force operations. It is also essential that they should operate within the law because the government must be able to take responsibility for what they do.

There are a number of different ways in which the British Army could be called upon to help a friendly government which was engaged in a counter-insurgency campaign. For example, it could merely be asked to give advice about how the campaign should be developed, or it might be persuaded to supply detachments of specialized troops, such as the SAS, to train local security forces or even to take part in covert operations. Alternatively, the British Army might be called upon to go further and provide certain supporting arms which the local government could not find from its own resources, for example signals or helicopters or engineers. Finally it might be required to provide one or more brigades of conventionally armed troops together with their logistic support. These troops might be asked to take on some specific task such as the guarding of government installations in order to free local forces, or border surveillance, or they might be given an area of the country with a view to conducting the full range of counter-insurgency activities, i.e. a mixture of offensive and defensive operations.

In any of these circumstances the first thing is that all concerned should understand how a counter-insurgency campaign should be run so that they can ensure that the British contingent is used in a worthwhile manner. The campaign itself would impose some strain on the army because the commitment would undoubtedly run on for months or years, as it has in Northern Ireland and in most of the other counter-insurgency campaigns which the United Kingdom has undertaken in the past. On the other hand, unless the insurgency was at such an advanced stage that the enemy had built up an army of all arms capable of fighting in the open, it would be easier to put together a force for this purpose than for fighting a limited war, because the requirement for logistic units and supporting arms would be so much less. The actual skills required are mainly those needed for the army's other commitments short of the full scale mechanized and armoured warfare of NATO's Central Region. For example, troops involved in fighting insurgents must be capable of conducting patrols and ambushes, setting up road blocks, carrying out surveillance, handling riots, guarding installations and being adept at the basic military manoeuvres of advance, attack, withdrawal and defence.

At this juncture it is worth mentioning briefly the problem so often referred to as international terrorism in order to see whether the army has any role to play in this field, especially as the whole subject is beset by confusion and misunderstanding.

The reason why the problem seems so difficult to resolve is largely because the terminology used is insufficiently well defined. As explained in the Introduction, terrorism is not a form of warfare, but a tactic that can be used in conjunction with any of the steps on the ladder of warfare as a whole. International terrorism must also be seen as a tactic that can be used in conjunction with different forms of war, rather than as a form of warfare in its own right. Once this point is understood it is not particularly difficult to work out what should be done about a particular incident. Failure to look upon it in this way is likely to have the same sort of result as would be achieved by a doctor who tried to treat spots without first discovering whether they were caused by chicken-pox, mosquito bites or an allergy to shellfish.

Thus, when confronted by an act of international terrorism the first thing to do is to analyse the background to it. For example, it might be caused by a deliberate act of policy on the part of a foreign government wishing to bring pressure to bear on another country or group of countries, choosing this form of attack rather than diplomatic or economic action on the one hand or an overt assault on the other. In this case the terrorist incident represents an attack of a sort by one country on another and is therefore a form of limited war albeit carried out at a very low level of intensity. Some might prefer to call it confrontation. It can be countered in whatever way seems most advantageous by the country suffering the attack, bearing in mind the nature of the hostile regime and its overseas backing if any, world opinion, the situation of friendly nationals in the hostile country, and so on. Possible courses of action could consist of purely defensive arrangements designed to make further attack less likely combined with diplomatic and economic action, or it could consist of fostering subversion or insurgency in the hostile country. It could even include an overt assault in the form of a raid by naval, air or ground forces designed to damage the enemy's potential for launching further terrorist attacks, or to inflict injury designed to frighten the people into causing its government to desist. The important thing in this case is to realize that the terrorism is a symptom of hostility on the part of a foreign state and to act accordingly.

A separate situation arises if the acts of terrorism are the by-product of an insurgency taking place in some other country. For example, if a country is conducting a campaign against insurgents, the insurgents might perpetrate acts of terrorism against the nationals or property of a third country which they considered to be sympathetic towards the government which they were trying to overthrow or at any rate hostile to their way of thinking. They might go so far as to do it to get publicity for their cause, even though the country whose nationals or property were attacked was not supporting their own government. In this case possible forms of reaction would differ from those mentioned in the first example since the enemy is not in this case a foreign state but insurgents within that state. For this reason it might be better to assist the country concerned in dealing with its insurgents with particular reference to preventing them or their supporters from getting supplies or making use of the country as a sanctuary and base for propaganda activities. It might be sufficient to let the insurgents know that any further hostile action on their part would have this effect. If, on the other hand, the country's interests would seem to be more closely linked with the insurgents than with their government, help could be offered to them on the understanding that they ceased their terrorist attacks: this would of course constitute a hostile act against the country in which the insurgency was taking place.

There are naturally many variations based on these two alternatives. For example the terrorist incidents could be the work of insurgents defeated in one country who are living as refugees in another country. In this case the host country must be persuaded to act effectively against the refugees unless they desist from their hostile actions and help may be offered in doing so. If the host nation fails to act effectively or refuses to accept help, it is itself acting in a hostile way and may even have to be regarded in the same light as the hostile country in the first example, although the political and practical difficulties facing it would obviously have to be taken into account. Many other examples can be worked out by the simple expedient of looking round the world as it is today with particular reference to the Middle East and Central America.

Two points are fundamental to the way in which incidents of this kind are handled. First, purely defensive measures such as the searching of baggage at airports though useful in themselves are never more than a palliative. As when handling insurgency, defensive operations designed to prevent the enemy from advancing his cause must be balanced by offensive operations designed to identify and neutralize those involved either by bribing them, threatening them or by destroying them. Second it is a mistake to go on record with a blanket condemnation of all acts of terrorism, since sooner or later groups with whom the country sympathizes and may even wish to support will be involved in committing them as they may have no other means of pursuing their aims. It is none the less important when trying to counter groups using international terrorist tactics to get countries to act together against them because such measures as cutting off aid and denying sanctuary only work efficiently when co-ordinated over a wide area.

With this as background it is easy to work out the sort of tasks which might be given to the army. For example, the army might have to help a country in dealing with its insurgents in the way described earlier, and by the same token it must be capable of helping insurgents overthrow their government should the need arise. A requirement to protect and evacuate British or friendly nationals along the lines mentioned earlier could also arise out of operations taken to discourage a country from instigating or supporting those involved in carrying out acts of international terrorism. In short, since international terrorism is not a form of war, but merely a tactic that could be met in the context of any form of warfare, the army's part in countering it would merely be part of its normal business in fighting the war concerned.

If the British Army was asked by a friendly country to help repulse an incursion from outside it could be involved in a full scale limited war, although not all incursions take that form. It is only necessary to remember how the Indonesian confrontation with East Malaysia developed in the 1960s to realize that there are many variations to the way in which one country can harass another. Indeed, because of the pressures that nuclear powers exert to discourage overt wars which could escalate danger-ously, covert forms of incursion based on encouraging and assisting home grown insurgents are, if anything, more likely to occur than straightforward invasion. Should British forces get drawn in to an operation of this type, the tactics used would have more in common with countering insurgency than with limited war and the force would have to be composed and equipped with this end in view.

If, however, the job is one of helping a friendly country to repulse an overt invasion, then the composition of the force and the method of operating would more closely resemble the sort of operations discussed in connection with the army's contribu-tion to the Northern Region of NATO, although the climate and terrain might be very different. Even so it is only necessary to draw the comparison to understand some of the major con-straints which would have to be overcome.

For example, if the enemy is equipped with tanks, can they be countered by tanks of the country being attacked, or by a combination of anti-tank missiles and air power, or must the British force take tanks? It will only be able to do so if the tanks can be delivered by sea since they are too big to go by air. If tanks are taken, the logistic element of the force would have to be considerably increased. A similar set of questions can be posed in relation to other components of the force such as air defence weapons. It is unusual for countries to have an air defence capability which is in excess of what it needs to cover the operations of its own forces. It would therefore be absolutely essential for a British force to take an adequate scale of air defence weapons with it. Unless it does so it would be totally incapable of manoeuvring in the face of enemy air action. A further problem relates to the amount of artillery that the force would need: clearly it would have to take its own direct support artillery and it would probably also have to take some heavier weapons in order to supplement the artillery resources of the country concerned so that the combined artillery force was adequate to support the additional troops provided by Britain. Answers to these points, together with many others, would dictate the overall size of the force that would have to be sent.

Even if tanks were not required, a force capable of undertaking a role of this sort would have to include a higher proportion of artillery, engineers and signals than one designed for countering insurgency and would in consequence be far more difficult to find and maintain overseas for any length of time. An even greater difficulty would arise in finding the necessary logistic units, since so many of those designed to operate in a European war come from the Territorial Army and would not therefore be available to take part in an operation outside the NATO area in peacetime. Indeed, unless an ally, or the country calling for help, was prepared to make up some of these shortfalls, it might be impracticable to respond to a call for assistance at all.

The next example relates to the situation where the country concerned was opposed to the introduction of British troops, either to look after British nationals, or to enforce a British interest. In this case the force would have to fight its way into the country or at best, if it managed to slip in by some unexpected and unguarded entry point, it would have to be ready to defend itself as soon as it arrived. Furthermore it could expect no logistic support from the country it had invaded and would therefore have to take all that it required with it. From an operational point of view the business of making an opposed entry into an enemy country could only be carried out by an amphibious landing or by the capture of an airhead using parachute units followed by rapid air-landed reinforcements, unless there was a friendly country bordering it which was prepared to allow its territory to be used as a springboard for the launching of a ground attack.

In order to mount an amphibious operation it is obviously necessary that there should be a coastline within striking distance of the target area. The next most important consideration is that the operation could only be mounted if it was possible to provide air cover capable of neutralizing the enemy's offensive air capability, always assuming that he has any. The last of the essential conditions is that the enemy should not be able to concentrate an overwhelming force against the troops that are landed in the time that it takes them to complete their job.

In order to mount an airborne assault on a hostile country, the first requirement is that there should be one or more mounting airfields within flying distance of the proposed airhead and that the countries over which the force must fly *en route* permit the overflight, or at least are unable to stop it. The next requirement is that the aircraft carrying the parachute troops should be protected from enemy attack whilst in transit and that the follow up aircraft should be similarly defended. The third requirement is that all the equipment which the ground forces need in order to repulse the enemy and achieve their aim can be carried in the follow up aircraft. Finally it must be possible to land a force that is large enough to avoid being overrun by the enemy.

In practice, despite the success of the assault on the Falkland Islands in 1982, it is unlikely that many situations involving an opposed landing in a hostile country could arise which would be within the capability of British amphibious or airborne forces to resolve on their own. None the less, the possibility exists and must be regarded as a commitment for the army. Taken together with the desirability of being able to provide a British element in an allied amphibious or parachute force, the commitment provides a justification for maintaining these capabilities that their usefulness in a European war would hardly justify because of their vulnerability to modern weapons. The usefulness of both amphibious and parachute forces in situations where a friendly country invites British troops in, provides additional cause for retaining them.

The final situation relates to the provision of a peace-keeping force, which has a totally different job to a force whose task is to counter insurgency, although this latter activity is often described as 'keeping the peace'. A peace-keeping force is one that is inserted between two or more parties to a dispute, with the consent of all of them, to help them find a solution to their differences by peaceful means. Peace-keepers are not supposed to use force except in self-defence, and even that should be unusual as they should never be attacked because they are supposed to be working for the benefit of all parties to the dispute. In practice they sometimes do find themselves under attack because of the action which they have to take in order to achieve their aims.

Peace-keeping is a highly specialized form of military activity which, since it cannot be based on the use of force, has to be based on a mixture of diplomacy, observation and bluff. If the opposing sides are negotiating they may well also be planning to take some military action in order to put themselves in a stronger negotiating position. Where the commander of the peace-keeping force feels that such action could result in a further outbreak of hostilities he may try and pre-empt it by, for example, occupying a piece of ground that he feels one of the sides intends to grab as a negotiating counter. Alternatively he may decide to establish himself in between them, in the hope of making it difficult for them to attack each other. There is an immense variety of activities which a peace-keeping force can undertake, and most of them include being in a position to know what the disputants are up to so as to be able to give an objective account of incidents, thereby nullifying the advantage which the instigator is trying to get by misrepresenting the way in which events have developed.

But every time the force succeeds in preventing one side or the other from making headway it appears to be helping the other side. If the peace-keeping force does its job properly it will soon find itself unpopular with both sides, and both sides will probably take action designed to handicap its activities. It is a short step from this position to one in which isolated 'unattributable' incidents start to occur, designed to warn off the peace-keeping force, or to prevent it from operating freely in a particular part of the country. Such activities are usually accompanied by a barrage of propaganda, officially deplored by the leaders of the side concerned, and directed against that part of the peace-keeping force which has been thwarting their machinations.

It has in the past been unusual for a peace-keeping force to be drawn from one nation only; they have usually been multi-national, because only by having a number of nations involved is it possible to persuade all the parties to a dispute that the force as

75

a whole will be impartial. Thus the commitment from the army's point of view is usually to provide a contingent complementary to that provided by other countries. The sort of units most favoured are infantry backed by light reconnaissance, engineers, signals and logistic units, together with some staff officers to work in the force headquarters. Although it is almost always difficult to produce units of any sort for any additional commitment, the way in which peace-keeping forces get put together by the international community does at least provide an opportunity to negotiate a contribution related to what is available at any given moment.

Only one other thing needs to be said about the commitment of peace-keeping which is that it is dangerous to send officers or soldiers to carry out this function unless they are properly trained for the job. As there is never enough time to teach people the business at the last minute, when a force is being put together, it is essential that the fundamentals at least should be taught to all soldiers as part of their normal training. The subject should certainly be included in all officer training courses from Sandhurst onwards, a point that is underlined by the knowledge that there has not been a single day for well over twenty years when some British officers have not been employed on peace-keeping duties. It is almost as likely a task for the army to be called upon to undertake as countering insurgency.

There is one other task outside the NATO area and that is providing garrisons for British possessions overseas. Although this commitment is now greatly reduced, there are still garrisons in Hong Kong, Cyprus, Gibraltar, Belize and the Falkland Islands. As the years go by some of these garrisons will doubtless be removed but some new ones may be required. The main implication of finding garrisons is the effect they have on overall army force levels and strengths. They also provide good training opportunities and an inducement to recruiting, because many people still join the army to see the world: not just Europe.

Having examined the sorts of task that the army might be called upon to undertake it is now worth trying to put them into a geographic context in order to get some idea of the scale of the operations that could ensue. In practice no one is ever able to foresee the future with any degree of accuracy, so this part of the examination should only be viewed as an attempt to illustrate the earlier part of the chapter.

At the moment the most dangerous areas in terms of causing a breakdown between the nuclear powers are the Middle East and South West Asia. The sensitivity of the West to a Russian inspired threat to the flow of Arab oil, and the support which the United States gives to Israel in its confrontation with the Arabs, provide plenty of opportunity for conflict. At present, the United Kingdom contributes to two peace-keeping forces in the area, one in Cyprus and one in Sinai, and has only recently withdrawn from a third in Beirut. British ownership of the Sovereign Base areas in Cyprus, with its attendant garrison commitment, partly results from these factors, as also does the British involvement in Oman where the army still provides officers to train and assist the Sultan's forces.

Almost every sort of overseas involvement for the British Army could crop up in this area. For example, there could be a call to evacuate British nationals from many of the countries, although the strength of their armed forces would make it almost impossible to carry out an opposed evacuation without the help of an ally. Alternatively the United Kingdom might agree to help a friendly country fight its insurgents as it has done in the recent past in Oman. It is also possible that Britain might be prepared to position a force in a friendly country threatened by an outside attack as a deterrent, although it would almost certainly have to be a tri-service force and not one found by the army alone. This happened in Kuwait in 1961. There are few places where Britain would be strong enough to do this now, other than in conjunction with an ally. The same considerations would apply to an even greater extent, if the country concerned was already under attack. A variation on this theme might be if the army was needed to secure a base in a threatened country for a British naval or air force. Finally it is just possible that the army might be required to take part in an opposed assault on a country that had been attacked and overrun by an aggressor, but there is nowhere in the Middle East where this could now be done other than in conjunction with an ally.

At the moment Africa is rather less sensitive than the Middle East and the involvement of Russia and America less direct. Few African countries other than South Africa can afford strong defence forces equipped with modern weapons and as a result in the post-colonial era they have seldom attacked each other directly. There have, on the other hand, been a large number of insurgencies in African countries, some of which have been instigated, exploited or assisted from outside. Some military help has been provided from outside the continent, for the benefit of governments and insurgents alike, but most of it has been in the form of equipment sold on favourable terms or of training assistance. Sometimes when the training assistance has taken the form of resident training teams these people have themselves become involved in insurgency or counter-insurgency operations.

In the future it is probable that the importance of certain parts of Africa both to Russia and to the West will increase as the economic stakes are raised and as rivalries between the post-colonial African powers become more marked. It is therefore probable that both sides will become more directly involved in their attempts to influence events to their advantage, especially as the dangers of escalation to nuclear conflict are considerably less than they are in the Middle East. Even if in the long term future the existing balance between Russia and America were to give way to some other form of confrontation, Africa with its great reserves of largely unexploited resources would still be important to the rival powers; and Britain would have to be allied to one of them. Even on her own account Britain has many economic interests in Africa.

The fact that a large number of British interests and British nationals are scattered about the continent, particularly in countries which were formerly part of the Empire, combined with the fact that a relatively small expenditure of military effort can make a considerable impact over much of the area, means that the army is certain to be involved there from time to time. Indeed this is now the case to the extent that Britain provides a significant number of officers to help train the armies of Nigeria, Uganda and Zimbabwe, together with smaller numbers in several other countries.

It is more difficult to predict the way in which events are likely to develop in Africa than it is in Europe, for example, because of its vast size and the many uncertainties that govern events there, particularly in the southern part of the continent. In terms of a contribution from the British Army, the options can be narrowed down to the extent that assistance is more likely to be asked for by countries that were formerly part of the British Empire than by others, although that consideration may become less in evidence as the years go by. By far the most effective form of help is that provided by training or advisory teams before something goes wrong, but it is possible that the British government would respond to a call for specialized units or even a small force to help a friendly country cope with insurgents, or with incursions from across its borders. Another likely use for British troops would be as part of a United Nations or Commonwealth peace-keeping force.

A major problem exists with regard to the use of British troops in Africa concerning the delivery of the force and its subsequent maintenance in the country concerned. This is not so much a matter of distance as of access and relates to the willingness of countries along the way to allow overflying rights and possibly refuelling facilities. Although these problems are not for the army to resolve, they do slightly reduce the probability of its being used and are therefore relevant to the priority which should be given to preparing the army for such adventures. There is at the moment a stock of goodwill towards the United Kingdom in a number of countries which would enable the movement of troops to be carried out, providing that the countries concerned did not disapprove of the object of the enterprise. Also in countries where there is no particular goodwill towards the United Kingdom, it might be possible to get overflying rights and transit facilities through the good offices of a third country which both approved of the purpose of the deployment and had influence with the country concerned. In short the ability to use military power in support of the national interest in Africa is as much dependent on the success of diplomacy as it is on the existence of adequately structured and prepared forces.

The likelihood of having to use the army in Central Asia or the Far East seems now to be much less than in the Middle East or Africa, with the principal exception of Hong Kong where a garrison already exists. Here it has to be accepted that reinforcements might be required in order to maintain the stability of the Colony up to the time of the ultimate withdrawal in 1997. There are also a small number of British troops in Brunei, but it is unlikely that this would lead to a significant extra commitment.

None the less the army could be involved in evacuating British nationals, or it could be asked to participate in a peace-keeping force almost anywhere in the area. It is even possible that it could be sucked in to helping the Americans in some more extensive operation in the context of a gradual change in the main power balance, but such a contingency is not likely to arise for some time yet. It is most improbable that the British Army would be called upon to maintain any significant capability over and above what it needs to carry out its commitments in Europe, the Middle East or Africa in order to undertake operations in the Far East.

The only other parts of the world worth mentioning are Central and South America since the army is already involved in both.

In Belize there is a garrison the purpose of which is to deter incursions from Guatemala and ensure the continued independence of the country. Troops went there in the first place to ensure the smooth transfer of the former colony to independence and the United Kingdom certainly did not envisage the commitment continuing for so long, as post-colonial problems in the area are normally handled by the United States; even it seems in Commonwealth countries! But it suits Belize and the United States, and probably even Guatemala, that the United Kingdom should continue to deploy troops in the country. While they are there the possibility must exist that they would have to be reinforced should Belize be attacked and the army, together with the other two services, has to be ready to undertake what would

80

be a considerable operation. Once British forces are withdrawn from the Caribbean it is not very likely that they would be required to return because of the predominant role of the United States in the area. Even so, they might conceivably have to operate with the Americans in order to demonstrate solidarity.

The British Army is also garrisoning the Falkland Islands and it is difficult to know how long this commitment will last. While it does, a capability to reinforce the islands and fight a comparatively sophisticated war there has to be retained. The fact that the commitment arose in the first place, and continues to this day, serves only to accentuate the fact that the most extraordinary and unexpected situations can arise, and that the services have to be ready to cope when the politicians and diplomats get in a muddle.

Part 2

PREPARATION REQUIRED

Chapter 6

TODAY'S ARMY

The purpose of the second part of this book is to establish the extent to which the army is capable of carrying out its commitments and to point out what needs to be done to overcome any shortcomings. In order to do this, the problem has to be examined on two separate levels. First there is the purely practical aspect of matching the resources which are likely to be made available to the commitments that are likely to crop up. Clearly the double uncertainty highlighted by the two uses of the word 'likely' makes this difficult enough to resolve and no attempt will be made to do so in a strictly mathematical sense. But there is an even more difficult and more important aspect of the problem, which is to establish whether the army as at present constituted is capable of working out what is required and then of making best use of whatever resources it can get hold of to meet its commitments. It is this aspect of the business which constitutes the main topic of the examination.

This chapter is designed to outline very briefly and in the broadest terms the sort of army that Britain now possesses. Subsequent chapters will relate this to the commitments, highlight the shortcomings and suggest how they should be overcome.

At the moment (1986) there are just over a quarter of a million people in the army, of whom approximately 172,000 are on full-time engagements.[1] This latter figure includes women as well as men and it includes people enlisted outside the United Kingdom, such as the Gurkhas. In addition to this, there are approximately 85,000 part-time soldiers belonging to the Territorial Army, the Home Service Force and the Ulster Defence Regiment, most of whom belong to units which could become operational at very short notice. All these people are members of the army and most of them are on the strength of units that exist in peacetime, that have a small regular component and that carry out training throughout the year.

Separate from these people, and not included in the quarter of a million, are a number of Individual Reservists who were at one time in the regular army and who retain an obligation to rejoin should the government call upon them to do so. Although not part of the army in peacetime, the contribution that they would make in the event of war would be of great importance. There are on paper around 153,000 of these people, divided into various categories, but it is unlikely that they would all be capable of useful employment.

Of the 172,000 full-time soldiers, approximately 26,000 are undergoing individual training away from units, e.g. as recruits or on long courses, and cannot therefore be counted against the numbers required to fulfil the army's commitments. Of the remainder about 60,000 are stationed in Germany (including Berlin) and another 11,000 in garrisons around the world. The rest are based within the United Kingdom, although at any given moment some may be deployed overseas for operational reasons.

Although an arithmetical calculation would indicate that the number of men and women remaining in the United Kingdom is high, it will be found that many of them are involved in carrying out support tasks or routine functions and cannot therefore be counted against the numbers needed to undertake or prepare for the commitments described in previous chapters. Furthermore, for the last seventeen years a state of insurgency has existed in Northern Ireland which has made a considerable demand on army manpower.

The main functional components of the army are the 'arms', such as the infantry, armoured corps, artillery, engineers and signals, and the logistic and administrative 'services', e.g. transport, ordnance and electrical and mechanical engineers. This list is not by any means exhaustive.

So far as the 'arms' are concerned, units, which are known as regiments or battalions, are composed mainly of men from one of them but often contain significant numbers from some of the 'services'. For example, an infantry battalion consists mainly of infantrymen but will also include members of the Royal Electrical and Mechanical Engineers to handle repair and maintenance, members of the Army Catering Corps to do the cooking, members of the Royal Army Pay Corps to handle the pay and so on. In units which rely heavily on technically complicated weapons or equipment, such as an air defence regiment, the number from outside the parent corps, in this case the artillery, would almost equal the rest. The biggest arm is the infantry which has 96 battalions (including 40 from the Territorial Army), followed by the artillery with 28 regiments (6 TA), followed by the armoured corps with 24 regiments (5 TA) and then the engineers with 20 regiments (7 TA).[2]

The same system of manning usually applies to units of the logistic services, i.e. they are based on one 'service' but contain members from the others as required: for example a Field Workshop, which is a unit of the Royal Electrical and Mechanical Engineers, would also have members of some of the other 'services' on its strength. Occasionally a mixed unit is formed from several of the 'services' such as the Logistic Battalion which serves the Allied Command Europe's Mobile Force.

A number of units from the infantry and the armoured corps grouped together make up the basic formation, which is a brigade. A brigade, backed by artillery, engineers, signallers and some units from the logistic services, is the standard grouping on which plans for carrying out many of the army's commitments are based. For example, the United Kingdom Mobile Force, which is held to reinforce NATO's Baltic Approaches, is a force of this sort. Often, however, two or more brigades operate together, in which case it may be convenient to form them into a larger group which can use the combined resources of the artillery, engineers, etc. for the benefit of both, or all, of them. This is what happened in the Falkland Islands campaign. Where plans exist for the permanent association of two or more brigades in this way, the resultant formation is known as a division. Divisions form the basis for planning in NATO's Central Region and all the British brigades stationed in Germany in peacetime, excluding the one in Berlin, are part of divisions. There is also one division in the United Kingdom which is earmarked for use in Germany in war. Altogether there are at the moment four divisions and twenty-six brigades in the British Army.

The availability of brigades together with logistic support is a better method of determining capability than a straightforward head count, although, of course, there is a great difference in capability between one brigade and another. For example, the armoured and mechanized brigades in Germany are equipped with main battle tanks and heavily protected armoured personnel carriers, whilst the brigades held in the United Kingdom that are designed to reinforce NATO hold lightly protected wheeled vehicles in some cases and soft-skinned vehicles in others according to their likely tasks. Another brigade in the United Kingdom whose main wartime role would probably be to act as the Commander-in-Chief's reserve, is organized as an air portable brigade and is therefore particularly suited to use outside the NATO area. Some of the other brigades in the United Kingdom are merely groupings of units for training purposes and have no logistic backing.

Undoubtedly one of the most important factors in determining the success of an army in war is the way in which the different 'arms' work together on the battlefield, and that depends to some extent on how they and units of the logistic services are grouped together within formations. It also depends on a number of other things, such as how the officers of the different 'arms' are trained and regard each other, and the way in which tactical doctrine is worked out for the army as a whole. Unfortunately the British Army has been particularly slow to learn this lesson, which is partly due to the emphasis placed on certain aspects of the regimental system, of which more later.

Most units from the 'arms' move every few years in order to widen their experience and skills. Thus an infantry battalion after being in the British Army of the Rhine for six years, would probably become part of a brigade in England for two years and then do a two-year tour with its families in Hong Kong or

Cyprus or Northern Ireland. Another battalion might spend longer in England during which time it could be sent to do a short tour of four or five months without its families in the Falkland Islands, or as part of the United Nations Force in Cyprus or on an emergency tour in Northern Ireland. The same sort of pattern would apply in the artillery, engineers or armoured corps, although the tour lengths would be different to take account of the balance of 'arms' in a particular place. For example, a regiment of the armoured corps would spend longer in Germany, because a much higher proportion of the armoured corps is wanted there than anywhere else.

No understanding of the British Army is possible without a realization of the disparity arising from the requirements of the different theatres in which it works. The training, equipment and lifestyle of a unit in Germany is totally different to that of one stationed in Great Britain or in Northern Ireland, or Hong Kong or the Falkland Islands. Furthermore, because it costs so much to maintain forces in Germany capable of carrying out their operational role and because it is so important to do this in terms of maintaining the solidarity of NATO, there is usually insufficient money left to keep the troops deployed in other parts of the world, particularly those in the United Kingdom, at a high enough state of readiness. From a financial point of view this statement is an oversimplification of a situation which embraces the Royal Navy and the Royal Air Force as well, but it is none the less valid in this context.

A few regiments with very highly specialized roles are stationed permanently in the same place, and the officers and men within them come and go, exchanging with people from other units. This provides for continuity and enables the individuals to widen their experience, but at some expense in terms of the cohesiveness of the unit and of *esprit de corps*. This system, known as trickle posting, is widely practised amongst the logistic services where it is the norm rather than the exception. It is also the system on which all training units, base establishments, depots and headquarter staffs are manned.

At the heart of the organization of the British Army is the regimental system which arose out of the way in which forces were put together even before the formation of the standing army in 1661. The method then adopted was that various prominent people would be made responsible for raising a regiment of infantry, or one or more troops of cavalry, to take part in a particular campaign. As a result, a good proportion of the men in these regiments or troops would come from the estates of the person who raised them and would therefore be bound together to some extent by loyalty to their master and to each other.

Out of this, a sort of regimental family feeling developed which has continued to exist to this day, although the original method of raising regiments has long been forgotten. It is this family spirit which results in each man being determined to avoid letting down his comrades in a crisis and it has been very successful in helping men to withstand the terrors of the battlefield. It can be fostered in many ways, but it only works if the group to which he belongs is small enough for each member to feel that the other members really are his comrades. Personal acquaintance, shared experience, operational successes, common items of uniform, a compact recruiting area or a record of the past achievements of the regiment, can all be used to foster this spirit, although none of them on their own is essential. A degree of discipline is, however, necessary in order to give individuals the strength to resist the overwhelming human instinct for self-preservation. But regardless of how the regimental system arose in the first place, or how it works now, it represents without question the greatest strength of the British Army today.

Originally the regimental system was developed within the infantry and the cavalry, because of the way in which troops of this sort were raised. Over the centuries the cavalry developed into the twenty-four regiments of today's armoured corps and the infantry regiments became divided into two battalions each, although some have now reverted to one and others have finished up with three. But regardless of these variations the groupings have remained small enough for the system to work.

The way in which the other 'arms' and the 'services' were incorporated into the army over a period of many years was doubtless influenced by their origins. For example, as recently as the Napoleonic wars, the artillery was provided by a separate department of state run by a politician known as the Master General of the Ordnance and the commissariat from which the logistic services have developed was a civilian organization responsible to the Treasury and therefore to the Prime Minister. With this background it is hardly surprising that the army has evolved along largely federal lines. As the other 'arms' and then the 'services' became incorporated into it, variations of the regimental system were developed to suit each of them, since the very close knit groupings of the infantry and cavalry were neither necessary nor did they fit their method of operating.

Thus many variations of the regimental system evolved under different names based on larger and looser entities than those adopted by the infantry or armoured corps. For example, although all the artillery in the army is known as the Royal Regiment of Artillery, it is in fact an 'arm' and not a regiment. Indeed, it is composed of twenty-seven different units also called regiments, although even these units do not work on the full regimental system, as the people in them are often trickle posted from one to another. Similar arrangements are used by the engineers and the signals, although these 'arms' describe themselves collectively as corps rather than regiments. The same system is also used by the logistic services. Each 'arm' and 'service' developed what might best be described as an extended family spirit in order to get some of the benefits of the full regimental system, and each was allowed a small headquarter staff to co-ordinate this aspect of life.

In a general sense command of the army is exercised from the Ministry of Defence to the Commanders-in-Chief in the United Kingdom and in Germany, thence down through the subordinate commanders of formations, e.g. divisions and brigades, to the commanding officers of the units. In a few cases it passes from the Ministry of Defence to a tri-service commander overseas, such as Commander British Forces Hong Kong or Cyprus, instead of to a Commander-in-Chief and there are other minor variations in the system to suit particular operational or administrative circumstances.

91

Ideally there should be no interference with the established chain of command, but in practice the various 'arms' often try to bring pressure to bear for the benefit of their own people. For example, they may press for the adoption of a particular weapon system knowing that it will enhance the size or importance of their 'arm', or they could use their influence to oppose a strategic option that would give less good opportunities for the use of their own 'arm', regardless of the fact that in both cases it is for the chain of command to make the decisions. In order not to get left behind in this scramble for power the infantry and the armoured corps also obtained co-ordinating headquarters despite the fact that they have a fully developed regimental system that does not need any addition of this sort to carry out normal regimental functions.

An understanding of the fact that the various 'arms' and logistic services bring influence to bear on the internal workings of the army is essential, since without it very little of the debate over commitments or the action necessary to meet them makes sense. This influence is not limited to official representations made by the 'arms' headquarters. Almost as important is the way in which officers grow up to look after the interests of their 'arms' when they reach positions of power. There are, of course, many advantages to be gained from the system in terms of the management of both officers and men and in the fostering of *esprit de corps*. Also the existence of many small groups exerting power in different directions provides a degree of robustness in an organization as large and complex as the army, so long as the whole is kept in balance: it is like the combination of atoms in a molecule. But equally the pressure which this system brings to bear on the chain of command sometimes hampers the making of correct decisions. In particular it puts a brake on any attempt to make radical changes and although this reduces the likelihood of disastrous decisions being made, it also prevents objective assessments of long term policies being put into effect.

It is an ironic fact that the fostering of an 'arms' consciousness, which is in effect a variant of the army's greatest strength, the regimental system, is the cause of many weaknesses including the frequent failure to combine the operation of all arms and services efficiently for the achievement of a common purpose.

The last point which needs to be mentioned in this brief introduction to the problems facing the British Army concerns the men and women who serve in it. The one thing which they have in common is that they all volunteered to join, but apart from that the variations in their terms of service and qualifications are almost limitless.

Ostensibly the biggest divide is between those who are on full-time engagements and those who are officially part-time soldiers, e.g. members of the Territorial Army or the Home Service Force or the Ulster Defence Regiment. But even here the distinction is not as clear cut as might be supposed. For example, most of the people in the Territorial Army are expected to do forty days' training a year but some of them do two or three times that amount and there are plenty who have no civilian job to distract from their commitment to the army. Although for financial reasons part-time soldiers are not encouraged to put in too many days' training, the units would not work properly unless some of them did. In practice a few including officers in key positions, might run up as many as 160 days per year. By contrast a full-time soldier in a routine administrative post in the United Kingdom taking many weekends off together with public holidays and his annual leave could do as few as 220 days: he might even have a part-time job as a taxi driver, night watchman, casual gardener, musician, etc. Furthermore, even in terms of military effectiveness some men in the Territorial Army are better trained and have more experience than some regulars, especially if they have had former service in the regular army. The difference between full-time and part-time soldiers is therefore mainly one of degree.

Inevitably the least well trained men in a unit of the Territorial Army are far less effective than their counterparts in a regular unit and as many of them leave after a very short time, they never reach any sort of acceptable standard. There are, of course, no set engagements in the Territorial Army and members come and go as they please. Thus Territorial units always contain a much higher proportion of men who are unready to go to war than regular units do and the mean level of their operational

93

readiness is understandably and properly very much lower. It is, therefore, most important that they should not be given tasks that are beyond their powers, despite their enthusiasm and apparent similarity to units of the regular army. Needless to say it is very tempting in peacetime to give unsuitable commitments to the Territorial Army because it is cheaper than maintaining extra regular units.

Within the regular army men and women known as other ranks, to distinguish them from officers, are recruited at about eighteen to serve for up to twenty-two years, in the knowledge that the majority of them will leave before the termination of a full engagement. In practice a large number only stay for three years and these are the people who fill the ranks with private soldiers. Most of the corporals stay for beween six and nine years with the warrant officers and sergeants coming from those who stay for the full engagement. The result of this system is that the men who are in the most actively engaged parts of a unit are those who are young enough to stand the physical strain of combat, i.e. they are between eighteen and thirty-two. None of the people who join at eighteen goes on beyond about forty, but there are always some who join later and who may therefore go on serving into their middle forties.

There is one major disadvantage to the present system. Despite the advantages of keeping men in the most actively engaged parts of a unit young, the heavy turnover is not conducive to maximum efficiency in the more technically complicated mechanized infantry battalions and armoured regiments in Germany. A similar difficulty arises in the supporting and logistic units such as those of the Royal Engineers, Royal Signals or Royal Electrical and Mechanical Engineers, but this is partly overcome by the simple expedient of establishing in these units a higher proportion of non-commissioned officers who tend to stay longer in the army; a solution which is less easy to apply in the fighting units because of the need to reserve rank for the exercise of command.

The position with regard to officers in the full-time army is rather different. Although there are a number who serve on short service commissions of varying lengths, the man who has a regular commission is assured of a career up to the age of fifty-five providing that he manages to qualify for promotion. In order to ensure that units are officered for the most part by people of approximately the same age as the men, i.e. up to the early forties, employment has to be found for a considerable number after they have finished their life in units and still have fifteen or so years to serve. A few of these men are needed as formation commanders and senior staff officers; the rest are used in manning the higher headquarters, including the Ministry of Defence, and to some extent in the training organization and the administrative units. In order to give these people a sense of purpose and achievement, backed by adequate material rewards, an elaborate hierarchy of appointments exists which enables them to go on getting promoted as they get older. This system has the incidental advantage of maintaining some reserve against the need for a rapid increase in the size of the army at the outbreak of a major war, but it makes the handling of business in peacetime wasteful and cumbersome.

In summary it can be said that the British Army at about a quarter of a million men strong is still a sizeable force. The close integration of full-time and part-time units within it is certainly one of its main sources of strength and an important factor in enabling it to function economically. For example, were it not for the Ulster Defence Regiment the regular army would have had to have been larger over the past sixteen years in order to carry out its peacetime commitments, and were it not for the Territorial Army it would have to be much larger all the time in order to be ready to carry out its wartime commitments. And whatever their shortcomings may be, there is no doubt that part-time units are very economic indeed compared with full-time ones.

The effective strength of the army as a whole lies in its fighting units and in the logistic and administrative 'services' that support them. As a result of the way in which it has developed over the years, the army consists of what can best be described as a federated collection of 'arms' and 'services' which not only provide it with its greatest asset, the regimental system, but also with some considerable weaknesses with regard to the way in which it runs, including the way in which its component parts operate together.

Both the full-time and part-time army are composed entirely of volunteers. Broadly speaking the terms of service of the soldiers are well suited to getting enough people of the right age into the right jobs and of disposing of them thereafter. This is not the case with officers.

Altogether the British Army is neither typical of other modern armies nor of those recorded in history, although this of itself does not mean that it is unsuited to its purpose. In a general sense regular units are composed of first class officers and men as a result of which they are well trained resolute and reliable. In recent years they have been tested over and over again in such diverse circumstances as the insurgency in Northern Ireland, the limited war in the Falkland Islands and in peace-keeping operations in Cyprus, Zimbabwe and the Lebanon and in every case they have performed better than could have been expected. It would be difficult to overstate the dedication with which the officers and men in these units have gone about their operational tasks and the thoroughness with which they have prepared for them.

On a less happy note, the higher direction of the army is less effective and wasteful, partly because of the existence of the dual chain of command described in this chapter and partly because of the way in which the Ministry of Defence and some of the higher headquarters are organized. This will be discussed later on. Fortunately the weakness is at the higher levels rather than in the units, since although good units can work wonders despite indifferent direction, the very best laid plans will be useless unless there are good units to put them into effect.

Notes

1 All manpower figures in this chapter are from the *Statement on the Defence Estimates 1986*, vol 2, HMSO.

2 *Statement on the Defence Estimates 1986*, vol 1, p. 73, HMSO.

Chapter 7

CAPABILITIES AND COMMITMENTS

This chapter is designed to show how the army measures up to the commitments described in Part 1 of this book. Throughout this examination, when thinking about the way in which any particular campaign is likely to be conducted, it is important to bear in mind the influence exerted by the existence of nuclear weapons, with particular reference to the current nuclear balance between America and Russia and the way in which this is likely to develop in the future. This is none too easy to do, since no war has yet been waged between countries possessing nuclear weapons. The nearest that anyone has come to it was the war which took place in 1973 between Israel on the one hand and Egypt and Syria on the other. In this case both sides were backed by nuclear powers and this had an important bearing on the way in which the campaign developed. But it is not a very close parallel to what would happen if NATO and the Warsaw Pact became involved in a war especially as the nuclear balance has changed considerably since 1973.

There can be little doubt that the army is better prepared to meet its commitments in the Central Region of NATO than any-where else, which is hardly surprising since the overriding importance of this task has been recognized for many years. The strength of the army's position here lies in the fact that the hard core of armoured and mechanized forces required for the defence of the sector allocated to the United Kingdom is stationed in Germany in peacetime. These brigades and divisions are manned by long term volunteer soldiers, highly trained for a particular and specialized form of modern warfare and equipped with the most expensive and sophisticated weapons and armoured vehicles.

But despite these advantages there are some formidable weaknesses to contend with. That nearly all of the armoured regiments and mechanized infantry are in Germany, does not alter the fact that much of the corps, together with an appreciable proportion of the units which operate behind the corps' rear boundary, have to cross the Channel, and move a significant distance thereafter, before they can be ready to carry out their tasks.

So far as the regular element of this reinforcement is concerned, the situation is not too bad because the units are fully formed and trained in peacetime and unless involved in some short term deployment overseas or in Northern Ireland, would for the most part be grouped in the formations with whom they would fight. These units would, however, be less well equipped for fighting an armoured or mechanized battle than their counterparts in Germany, because they would be carried in lightly armoured wheeled vehicles rather than in full scale armoured personnel carriers.

So far as the Territorial Army units are concerned, the situation is less satisfactory because they would have to be called out and moved as soon as they were assembled. In the worst case they would have to be ready to fight as soon as they arrived. There would be no period of grace in which to shake down as was the case in 1939. A few Territorial units have tasks within the forward divisions and they could find themselves engaging the enemy within hours of their arrival. The majority have tasks further to the rear so they might have a little longer before being committed to battle, but this would not be the case if the enemy landed troops behind the forward divisions from helicopters or by parachute in conjunction with their initial assault. Although it is impossible to predict the course of the battle with any certainty, it is highly likely that these units would be engaged in intense and sustained operations at an early stage, which is asking a great deal of part-time soldiers, however good they may be.

98

When considering the length of time that British troops could continue fighting in the Central Region, it is as important to look at the facilities which exist for supplying and maintaining the units as it is to look at the fighting capacity of the units themselves. The NATO ruling is that all national contingents should hold sufficient stocks to enable their troops to sustain operations for thirty days, but no one can know exactly what is required for that purpose. Furthermore the stocks are no good unless they can be moved by logistic units to the right place, and in addition to this, equipment has to be repaired and maintained and casualties have to be dealt with. So much is uncertain in this field that it is impossible to know whether the arrangements made by the United Kingdom are keeping up with ideas about how long operations must be made to last in terms of gaining time to negotiate before nuclear weapons are used. All that can be said is that the British are probably as well placed as most of the other national contingents.

Another imponderable relates to the extent to which British officers and men would be capable of carrying out sustained operations on a modern battlefield. This is an area where things have changed very markedly in recent years as a result of the introduction of equipment that enables people to see and fight in the dark. The effect of this, combined with the aggressor's need to grab as much ground as possible for bargaining purposes, is likely to be that operations will be sustained throughout the twenty-four hours, so the lull which used to descend on the battlefield at night may be a thing of the past. Although such devices have been coming into service over a long period, there have been no full scale wars yet in which they have been tested.

But even if operations are not continued throughout the twenty-four hours, they are likely to be more intense than any that have happened in the past because of the need to achieve the maximum before the onset of nuclear war or a ceasefire. For this reason the demands that would be made on officers and men would be of unprecedented severity. Furthermore they would come at the very start of the war; there would be no time to replace weak links in the chain. Any notion that the less robust members of society could be replaced at the start of a war is unrealistic. From the description of the army given in the last chapter it can be seen that whereas most of the officers and men in a fighting unit should just be capable of coping with the strain, the same can hardly be said of the higher commanders and especially of the more senior staff officers. So far as these officers are concerned, present arrangements could not stand up to the ultra intense operations that are likely to develop on NATO's Central Front.

There are obviously other shortcomings in the army's ability to handle the Central Region commitment, although on the whole the British contribution in this area compares favourably with that of any other country at present. But new circumstances are always arising and it is important that they are constantly watched and analysed. For example, so far as the future is concerned one of the most important things is to ensure that advancing technology is correctly assessed. At the moment NATO as a whole rightly lays great store on the efficacy of the main battle tank, and its tactics and the composition of its formations bear witness to the fact. But it only needs a relatively small swing in favour of anti-tank weapons to change the whole basis of the alliance's operational concepts, which would in turn result in the need for differently composed formations. Indeed, without a war to test the balance of weapons, it is difficult to know when that moment has arrived. History is littered with examples of armies being destroyed merely because they had not correctly assessed such a change. Despite improvements in the armour of tanks, the advent of new anti-tank missiles together with the development of artillery shells which can home in on individual targets such as tanks and armoured personnel carriers and similar improvements in rockets fired by aircraft and helicopters means that the end of the present era of armoured and mechanized warfare may be in sight. What will follow and how the change will take place is difficult to predict as also is the timing.

But there is little doubt that change is on the way and that within a measurable period the tank and the armoured personnel carrier will yield up some of their predominance, possibly to artillery and helicopter-borne infantry. If this were to happen, the whole balance between the arms would need to be altered and the alteration might have to take place at considerable speed. The effect that this would have on tactics, weapon procurement and the whole business of resource allocation would be immeasurable. For the moment, however, the army would seem to be adequately prepared to carry out its commitment in the Central Region subject to the reservations mentioned.

The situation is different when it comes to the army's commitment to NATO's Northern Region, with particular reference to the Baltic Approaches where the main army responsibilities lie. Regardless of whether the force is deployed to Schleswig-Holstein or to Zealand, the biggest drawback is that none of it is there in peacetime and must therefore be moved in from the United Kingdom before it can start its operational deployment. Although the more senior commanders have the opportunity to visit the ground and although troop exercises are held there at regular intervals, there is nothing like the degree of understanding of the operational tasks that there is in the Central Region.

Apart from this, there is one advantage to deploying troops in the Northern Region, together with a number of other disadvantages. The advantage, and it is a big one, is that in Schleswig-Holstein and in North Norway the country is much better for defence than is the case in the Central Region, so that a less expensively equipped force can play a more useful role. This is because the force needs to be less heavily mechanized. This does not apply to the same extent in Zealand, although there is a different and even greater advantage to the defence there in that the enemy can only arrive by being landed from the sea or the air.

The first of the disadvantages is that the logistic backing of that part of the army earmarked for use in the Baltic Approaches is largely found by the Territorial Army, and although the logistic units of the Territorial Army are first rate, they still have to be called up and assembled before they can move and this would have the effect of increasing the time it would take to make the whole force ready for battle. It would also prevent the force from deploying in a period of rising tension before the outbreak of hostilities unless the government was prepared to call out the Territorial Army which it might not want to do for fear of appearing provocative.

The next disadvantage lies in the fact that the force does not know in advance which of the deployment options it will be asked to adopt. It cannot therefore prepare itself on the basis of a single clear plan for the opening stages of the war. In some ways this is no bad thing because it ensures that there is more flexibility built into the training programme, but the disadvantages in terms of the way in which the force is made up and the problems concerned with its logistic support outweigh this advantage.

Certainly the force earmarked to go to the Baltic Approaches is less well found than that earmarked for use in the Central Region. If it went to Zealand it would be under-armoured and under-mechanized for the sort of battle that must be expected, and whichever option was adopted the force would probably find itself short of air defence facilities, although this matter has to be seen in relation to the overall air situation prevailing, rather than in terms of the air defence facilities which it takes with it. The number of fighting units which could be spared for use in the rear areas is also open to question, but again this is not entirely a matter of what the force takes with it since a lot would depend on the arrangements made by the Danes or the Germans.

In Northern Norway the situation is rather different in that the commitment is less firm. If all, or part, of the joint United Kingdom/Netherlands Amphibious Force was deployed there it would constitute a smaller proportion of the total allied force than would the British contribution to the defences of Zealand or Schleswig-Holstein. Also there is no doubt that the Amphibious Force is superbly trained for operating in this very exacting area. None the less it is not ideally composed for dealing with a threat which would probably be based on helicopter assault and it would almost certainly find itself short of air defence artillery and probably of field artillery as well.

In short, the army is not as well capable of carrying out its commitments in the Northern Region as it is in the Central Region because less priority has been given in this direction.

There is no doubt that the United Kingdom enhances the overall effectiveness of the alliance by undertaking to become involved in the area and there is equally no doubt that whatever force was sent in the event of war would be able to make a useful contribution. But a limited amount of adjustment in planning where the force should operate, together with a moderate enhancement to the force itself, would greatly affect its ability to make a successful contribution to the outcome of operations and would incidentally increase the chances of the force surviving the battle. The comments made with regard to the ability of officers and men to withstand the pace of operations apply just as much to operations in the Northern Region as they do in the Central Region.

The next thing to consider is the extent to which the army is capable of carrying out its commitments within the United Kingdom itself and there are three separate situations that require examination. The first is the help which the army may be asked to give to the police in countering subversion or insurgency in an otherwise peaceful period. The insurgency which has been going on in Northern Ireland for the past seventeen years is a good example of this. The second is the action which the army would be required to take in the period immediately leading up to the outbreak of a major war. The third is the action that would be required during such a war.

There is no doubt that the British Army is at present well qualified to deal with most of the likely commitments arising out of the first of these situations. The training which soldiers undergo to prepare them for operations in Northern Ireland, to say nothing of the experience which they get when they are there, means that they are very well capable of carrying out this task. Furthermore the fact that the army consists entirely of volunteers greatly strengthens its hand in resisting the inevitable propaganda directed at it when it becomes involved, and the standard of discipline which can be imposed on a volunteer army enables the soldiers to withstand the provocation to which they are always likely to be subjected in a campaign of this sort. So far as numbers are concerned there is a problem in terms of what could be made available quickly, but in an emergency troops could be diverted from Germany to cover the time in which more were being raised and trained.

There is, however, one important weakness, which is that the army no longer retains all of the specialist skills needed to maintain essential civilian services, such as the power stations, railways, or the sewerage system, should they be disrupted. Although some people object to the army having these capabilities, because possession of them would strengthen their hand in dealing with industrial disputes which have nothing to do with subversion or insurgency, it is none the less true that unless the army or the police have the ability to keep essential services going in an emergency the government may not be able to resist certain forms of genuinely subversive pressure. In this matter, as in so many others, the army must be ready to carry out its likely tasks and it is up to the democratically elected government to ensure that it does not use the army for improper purposes. It is also worth mentioning that the possession of these capabilities could be useful should the army be required to help an overseas ally in counter-insurgency operations.

The question of whether the army is capable of meeting its commitments within the United Kingdom during the period immediately prior to the outbreak of a major war is far more difficult to assess, especially as it would be hard to know when such a period had started.

It would seem likely that the first indications of trouble would come in the form of increased tension between Russia and the West, in which case there would probably be a rise in the number of rallies and demonstrations held by the various pressure groups, each trying to plug their particular view as to how the crisis should be handled. At the start of such a period the strength of the regular army in the United Kingdom would presumably be at its peacetime level, so there would be a fair number of troops available to help the police should they require assistance in handling the demonstrations or, alternatively, in doing other police tasks in order to free police to handle the demonstrations. But it could happen that the rising tension was itself due to a limited war overseas involving British troops, possibly in conjunction with American forces, in which case there would, of course, be fewer troops in the country.

If the tension continued to rise, some of the regular troops earmarked for the reinforcement of NATO might have been moved to the Continent, possibly under the guise of an exercise, and this would also reduce the numbers available in the United Kingdom. Throughout such a period no one would know if or when the storm would break. On the other hand military commanders would be acutely aware of the fact that guards for key installations would have to be in position before the onset of hostilities, because the installations would be at their most vulnerable shortly before the Russians launched their main overt attack. Once it was clear that war was inevitable, the Territorial Army and the Individual Reservists would be called out, which would greatly ease the problem of finding static guards, but the government might be reluctant to do this sufficiently early.

It is probable that in a period of acute tension the level of demonstrations would fall off as individuals closed ranks against the danger. This would obviously ease the army's commitment towards helping the police in this direction, although the police might then need help in controlling traffic if mounting fear caused a lot of extra civilian road movement. Again the army would be in a much better position to help once the Territorial Army and the Individual Reservists had been called up.

In summarizing the army's ability to meet its commitments in the United Kingdom in the period immediately before the outbreak of a major war, it can be said that in the best case, that is to say one in which the country was not involved in a limited war overseas or in providing major assistance to the police at home, the army would be able to do what was required of it. If on the other hand events turned out less favourably, there could be a shortage of troops at this critical time which might oblige the government to delay the despatch of some of the regular reinforcements to NATO for a few days to cover the call out of the Territorial Army and the Individual Reservists. This risk could be overcome by increasing the size of the army, by withdrawing from certain NATO commitments or by arranging for certain sections of the Territorial Army to be mobilized in advance of the main call out.

It is now time to examine the army's ability to meet its commitments within the United Kingdom during a major war and it is immediately apparent that there are many weaknesses to be overcome in this respect, in addition to the problem of the timing of call out for the Territorial Army, which has already been covered. On the other hand there are also some assets to be taken into account and it is worth enumerating these as a start, if only to indicate that the situation is by no means hopeless.

Undoubtedly the best thing that has happened in recent years is that the need for the army to do more than mount static guards on key installations has been recognized and a concept of operations has been formulated, as described in Chapter 4, which provides a good basis for development. In addition a framework of command facilities and communications has been set up which, although still very far from being complete, would at least enable commanders to work in conjunction with the civil authorities. In particular it would enable the forces to obtain vital resources from the civil community when needed, such as vehicles and aircraft. Finally, whilst assets are being counted, it is worth remembering that there are always likely to be a considerable number of American troops in transit through the country who could presumably be employed in a major emergency.

Against this, the most obvious weakness is the overall short-age of manpower and the poor state of preparation of most of the forces that would be available, both in terms of their standard of training and of the way in which they are equipped. Enthusiasm is a wonderful quality but it cannot make up for all other deficiencies, least of all for a deficiency of people to be enthusiastic.

In terms of infantry, even after mobilization and the redeployment needed to get the least well trained men doing the static guards and the better trained men doing the mobile tasks, there will still be a considerable overall shortfall. Although it is possible to establish the scale of this mathematically in terms of guarding the installations, it is impossible to do so in terms of the numbers that are needed to be held in reserve at every level because it is impossible to guess how the situation is likely to

106

develop. But it is these reserves or reaction forces on whom success depends, because they are the people who answer the calls for assistance from the installation guards or the civilian authorities and they are therefore the agents for restoring the situations that arise, whatever they may be. Leaving invasion out of account it would seem optimistic to suppose that the infantry component of the 100,000-odd men and women of all three services mentioned in the *Statement on the Defence Estimates 1986* quoted in Chapter 4 could possibly cope with the commitment. For practical purposes it is probably true to say that if the current infantry strength, including members of the Royal Navy and the Royal Air Force acting as infantry, was doubled there would still be a shortage.

So far as rectifying this position is concerned, the best way to increase the number of low category infantry capable of carrying out static guards is to continue enlarging the new Home Service Force. Because its members are required to train for so few days each year it is cheaper to maintain than the Territorial Army, but it must none the less be adequately equipped. To increase the infantry strength still further, it would be possible to raise auxiliaries within each company of the Home Service Force whose job in war would be to put in so many hours per week, i.e. they would be drawn from people who were doing some other necessary job which would preclude them from being called up for full-time service. They would in effect be like the Home Guard in the Second World War. The limitation to both of these measures is that it is no good raising forces unless it is possible to arm them and train them. Until the resources are available for doing this it is better not to recruit, because if a volunteer turns up to give of his time and finds that it cannot be profitably used, he will become discontented and depart, probably for good. Another matter that has to be considered is that the civilian authorities should also be trying to recruit people to help in handling casualties caused by bombing or to provide auxiliary firemen, etc. and it would not be helpful for the army to suck in all the available men and women without regard for the needs of civilian organizations.

In order to raise more infantry capable of carrying out mobile tasks it is necessary either to enlarge the Territorial Army even further, or to release some of the regular or Territorial Army units now earmarked for NATO reinforcement.

Leaving the question of a major amphibious raid or invasion out of account, there is still a clear need for armoured reconnaissance and engineer units in order to deal with the after effects of air attack or of action by enemy special forces. There is also a case for having some artillery units available for use in the air defence role. Although the main air defence of the country is clearly a matter for the Royal Air Force, it would be dangerous not to have some ground based weapons to cover the movement of troops which the enemy was trying directly to disrupt.

Under present arrangements there would be a distinct shortage of armoured reconnaissance and engineer units in the country once the reinforcement of Europe was completed, although there would be some capacity in these respects. In terms of reconnaissance there would be a number of unarmoured units, together with the reconnaissance elements in infantry battalions which would go some way towards filling the gap. There would be little difficulty in raising additional reconnaissance or engineer units within the Territorial Army but it would be a much more expensive thing to do than increasing the size of the low category infantry.

The same considerations apply to the artillery and throughout the logistic and administrative services, all of which would be in very short supply in the United Kingdom once the reinforcement of NATO was complete.

One further point with regard to the army's ability to carry out its role within the United Kingdom in war must be made which concerns chemical attack. Unless an agreement can be reached with the Russians which would result in all chemical weapons, together with the capacity for producing them, being destroyed, all military units and the civilian population must be made capable of defending themselves effectively against chemical attack as was the case at the outset of the Second World War. The only other alternative is for NATO to develop a full retaliatory capacity to act as a deterrent. If none of these steps is taken it could well be that a war, which might otherwise have been stopped before nuclear weapons were used, finishes up as a disaster for mankind, thus nullifying the effort and expense that has gone into defence over the past forty years.

It is difficult to summarize the ability of the army to meet its commitments in the United Kingdom in a major war. In the very best situation, that is to say one in which the war stopped before the Russians were capable of mounting a large amphibious raid or invasion and in which NATO air forces prevented any serious damage being inflicted by conventional, or nuclear attack from the air, then the army could probably safeguard important installations and provide such assistance as might be required by the civilian community. If, on the other hand, any of these provisos were not met, then the army would find it hard to meet its commitments. In short, in an area where almost anything might happen, there is barely enough capacity to deal with the most favourable situation; and although some of the other possibilities are relatively unlikely, some are all too likely to occur, particularly with regard to the damage which could be inflicted on the country by enemy air attack. Although the limitations in the army's ability to operate within the United Kingdom in war must be set against its shortcomings in other directions and against shortcomings in the capacity of the Royal Navy and the Royal Air Force to meet their commitments, it is pretty obvious that some action is needed to improve the situation. Luckily a lot can be done at relatively little cost and indeed a lot has been done in recent years.

The army's ability to meet the commitment of providing a force to operate outside the NATO area is the last problem that needs to be examined in this chapter. It can conveniently be covered by looking at the way in which the various components can be found and then checking on the extent to which they are organized, trained and equipped to carry out their likely roles. Providing that there was no embargo on using infantry held in the United Kingdom as reinforcements for NATO, there would be little difficulty in providing as many battalions as could be moved to, and supported in, the theatre of operations. On the other hand there would be a considerable penalty in doing this, especially if they had to be maintained overseas for any length of time, and an even greater penalty if they had to be relieved at the end of a few months, as would almost certainly be the case since they would have left at short notice in the first place. This arises from the fact that only enough infantry battalions are held to carry out foreseeable operations overseas, and most of the situations that materialize will probably be unforeseen. To provide extra infantry at short notice would involve interfering with the planned conversion of battalions from one role to another and their normal movement from one theatre to another. The net result would be increased instability especially for the families, an increased workload for the soldiers and a reduction in the state of training of formations in Germany, although this would be more than compensated for by the excellent training and operational experience gained by the units concerned, much of which would rub off on the army as a whole over a period. If the overseas commitment lasted for any length of time it might well become necessary to raise some extra battalions.

The same general considerations would apply to the provision of engineers and signallers as apply to the infantry, although in the case of signallers there is an overall shortage which might prove difficult to overcome regardless of penalties. In any case, because the total number of engineer and signal units in the army is less, the repercussions would be more noticeable.

The same general considerations would also apply to the finding of field artillery units, although there might be a problem regarding the weapons with which they were equipped. For example, artillery units designed to reinforce the Central Region of NATO are equipped with weapons that might well be larger than was desirable for the operation concerned because of limitations on the means of moving them or the ammunition. A rapid conversion to a lighter weapon would therefore have to take place at the last moment. A far greater problem would arise regarding the provision of air defence artillery because of the very small number of regiments available in the army as a whole, especially those equipped with weapons suitable for an operation outside the NATO area. Fortunately the artillery is one of the best trained and most efficient parts of the army and is capable of great flexibility when it comes to rapid conversion from one equipment to another.

Until recent years the provision of a force headquarters and headquarters for any brigades deployed would have proved difficult. Now, for a number of reasons this difficulty has been rectified as far as the brigade headquarters are concerned; several could be made available at short notice and one even specializes in the role. Plans also exist for putting together a higher level force headquarters at short notice from people who are earmarked in advance and who are assembled and trained together on exercises from time to time.

By far the biggest limitation would be in the provision of logistic units since so many of those earmarked to support NATO reinforcements come from the Territorial Army and would not therefore be available for an operation outside the NATO area in peacetime. Most of the regular field logistic units are in Germany in peace and could not be removed because they are needed to support the peacetime existence of the troops there: base logistic units are so heavily staffed by civilians that they would not be capable of being despatched on an overseas expedition of the sort envisaged.

It is not possible to be exact about the extent to which this factor would limit the army's ability to undertake an overseas operation because so much would depend on circumstances, such as the distance from the sea or air point of entry into the country to the place where the force was operating. Other logistic limitations would include the availability of stocks of ammunition, fuel, rations and other day to day requirements. Some of the shortfall might be made up by an ally or by the country where the operations were taking place, but if this were not possible then the logistic factor would undoubtedly limit the size of the force that could be deployed.

Altogether it might seem as if the army's ability to meet its commitments outside the NATO area is small in relation to the sort of situations that could arise, and this is indeed the case so far as limited war is concerned. But the same holds true of the Royal Navy and the Royal Air Force and since, in most cases, the army could not even get to the theatre of operations without

111

the help of the other services, it would not be worth having a capability that could neither be deployed nor supported. Without an effective ally, little more than a Falkland Islands type of operation could be attempted at short notice, although even this could be of considerable national value.

On the other hand the army would be better placed to help a friendly government in countering insurgency, since logistic limitations and shortages of air defence artillery, and support from the Royal Navy and Royal Air Force would be less of a limiting factor. Judging by current trends and past experience, this is the most likely overseas commitment to crop up with the possible exception of peace-keeping, and in this field also the army should have no difficulty in meeting its likely commitments.

One final point needs making with regard to the army's ability to carry out its commitments outside the NATO area and that concerns the training required. So far as limited war is concerned there is a lot in common with the training needed for carrying out the NATO commitments in the Northern Region and even some things in common with the training needed for operating in the Central Region, for example the basic infantry skills involved in holding ground. But much of the armoured and mechanized warfare skills necessary for the Central Region battle will be irrelevant in terms of overseas operations and indeed the lifestyle of troops who have been stationed for long periods in Germany is not ideally suited to preparing them for the more primitive conditions likely to be encountered overseas. It is, therefore, most important that units in the United Kingdom should receive rigorous and relevant training to fit them for the role.

Training for counter-insurgency is a totally different matter and in this case it is the training and experience of operations in Northern Ireland that is so valuable. On the other hand no two counter-insurgency campaigns are the same and it is important that officers in particular should study the subject carefully throughout their careers. It is extremely difficult for an army which has so great a preoccupation with armoured and mechanized warfare to concentrate sufficiently on this subject, but as it is far more likely to crop up, and as action in the early stages of a counter-insurgency campaign may well condition events for years to come, it is of the greatest importance that all concerned have a clear understanding of the issues involved. At the moment they do not.

Very much the same can be said of the training and officer education needed to prepare units to take part in peace-keeping operations, except for the fact that the consequences of not doing the job well are usually far less serious than in the case of countering insurgency. None the less, it is a form of military operation that is quite different from anything else and it is one that has to be learnt. It is also worth bearing in mind that the government would not incur the expense of deploying troops on a peace-keeping operation unless it was in the interest of the United Kingdom that peace should be restored and maintained in the country concerned. It is therefore of some importance that the troops deployed should know what is required of them.

To strike a balance across the whole spectrum of the army's commitments is no easy business, but it must be attempted. In the broadest sense it is probably fair to say that the army is capable of meeting its peacetime commitment in the Central Region of NATO both with regard to playing its part in deterring the Russians and in the more demanding business of satisfying the Germans that NATO provides their best form of defence at the moment. There is no doubt that these two functions constitute the most important single aspect of Britain's defence because they are fundamental to securing the support of countries that are powerful enough to safeguard her existence. The only other part of Britain's defence effort that is of comparable importance is the maintenance of an effective nuclear deterrent capability because that is the insurance against changes in existing alliances in the future.

But despite the fact that the army is playing its part in deterring the Russians and reassuring the Germans there are many weaknesses in the British contribution such as the problems of deployment on the outbreak of war and the standard and equipment of some of the reinforcing troops. Of these weaknesses the

113

one that stands out is the likelihood that the direction of operations above unit level would not stand up to the pace of modern war, because the more senior officers are too old. These, or similar weaknesses, are widespread amongst the other NATO contingents and do not therefore detract greatly from the credibility of the British contribution, although they would affect its performance in the event of war.

Weaknesses in the army's ability to meet its commitments in the Northern Region and in its ability to conduct limited war operations outside the NATO area are more marked than they are in the Central Region and they have a lot in common. The two most obvious shortages which affect both are air defence artillery and regular logistic units. Even if the will existed to make good these shortcomings, it would be very expensive to do so. In the case of the logistic units there is another hurdle to be overcome which is that politicians and some soldiers equate them with what they describe as 'tail' in contrast to fighting units which they describe as 'teeth'. From a military point of view this is absurd, since without a proper proportion of logistic units the fighting units can do nothing. But psychologically the view has some merit in that it reflects a very proper feeling that there is, somewhere in the army, an element of waste or fat which needs to be removed. This is true, but it is not the logistic and administrative units that constitute the fat so much as the overstaffing of the higher headquarters and the Ministry of Defence.

The problems regarding improving the army's ability to operate in the Northern Region of NATO, or outside the NATO area, could easily be resolved if the resources could be made available, but of course they could only be made available at the expense of something else, or if more money overall was to be devoted to defence.

By comparison, there would be few practical difficulties in improving the army's ability to take part in counter-insurgency or peace-keeping operations since the only requirement in the first instance is better training. If, however, a number of units were to be deployed for any length of time, the overall strength of the army would have to be increased, which would again involve additional resources.

114

Shortcomings in the army's ability to carry out its commitments with regard to the defence of the United Kingdom in peace and war are of a different order. To put them right requires not only an infusion of resources but, more important, a complete reassessment of the importance of the country's security not only within the United Kingdom itself, but also by the other NATO powers, with particular reference to the Americans and the Germans. Only if they become convinced of the relevance of the defence of the United Kingdom to their own security will it be politically possible for sufficient resources to be made available. The difficulty is that it is only in recent years that the security of the United Kingdom has become important to them and although the Americans may realize it, the Germans for the most part do not. It has come about as a result of the shift in the nuclear balance and the consequent need for the alliance to be able to fight for a longer period than was previously thought possible, a period throughout which the actual land mass of the British Isles will have an important part to play as described in Chapter 4.

The measures which need to be taken are fairly straightforward. They include a major increase in the number of lightly trained troops capable of guarding static installations so that better trained units of the regular and Territorial Army can be held together in proper formations capable of handling the many and varied situations that may arise. They also include establishing a proper balance of 'arms' and 'services' to enable these formations to operate. In short the needs of the defence of the United Kingdom should be worked out on their merits and the required action taken.

In weighing up the army's ability to carry out its commitments across the board, it would probably be true to say that although it is well placed to cope with the situation that existed in the early 1970s, it needs a certain amount of adjustment to enable it to manage events as they are today and a good lot more to be ready to deal with the situation that is likely to arise between now and the end of the century. On the other hand, despite the fact that many of the senior commanders and staff officers are too old, the army is soundly based, its regiments and corps are immensely professional and they are composed of officers and men who are devoted to their jobs in a way that is seldom found in foreign armies or indeed in many civilian organizations.

The difficulty in making the adjustments required is partly a matter of finding additional resources and in this respect a major problem arises from the fact that so much has to be devoted to the armoured and mechanized forces in Germany to enable them to do their job properly. As the Central Region commitment is quite different to all the others the money spent on much of the equipment required there and the research necessary for producing it and the training needed for using it, do not have a commensurate value in preparing units for any of the other functions that they may have to carry out. In fact, it is not only in the field of resources that this split between the needs of the forces in Germany and those stationed elsewhere becomes apparent: to some extent it has implications throughout the whole field of manning, training and the structure of the army itself.

Having established the problems which the army is facing in meeting its commitments, it is now possible to consider how they can be overcome.

Chapter 8

POLICY AND RESOURCES

A few of the army's shortcomings as described in the last chapter could be put right at little or no extra expense. This would apply, for example, to altering the age and career structure of the officers or adjusting some of the training priorities. But most of them could only be rectified by the allocation of significant extra resources.

The aim of this chapter is twofold. First it is to outline the system used for arriving at defence policy and to see whether any further alteration to it should be made in order to ensure that resources are allocated as effectively as possible. Second, to show what is involved in providing extra resources to overcome shortages in the army's ability to carry out its commitments.

Before 1982 each of the three services was separately charged with working towards the achievement of national defence objectives. The individual responsibility of the Royal Navy, the Army and the Royal Air Force was of fundamental importance and each had what was, in effect, its own separate headquarters in the Ministry of Defence, known as a department, headed by its own minister. The function of the Secretary of State for Defence, the Chief of the Defence Staff and the Permanent Under Secretary was to co-ordinate the formulation of defence policy in conjunction with the political and service heads of each of the single service departments. The service departments would then instruct their own Commanders-in-Chief as to their tasks and give them the resources which they would need in order to fulfil them. Co-ordination between the services outside the Ministry of Defence was achieved by the establishment of Commanders-in-Chief's Committees for specific tasks such as home defence or the mounting of operations outside the NATO area. This description is an oversimplification to some extent because there were certain activities such as the procurement of equipment and the research necessary for developing it which were handled on a tri-service basis, but on the whole it gives a fair indication of the arrangements which existed before 1982.

This system was set up in 1964 when the three separate service ministries were concentrated under one roof as the Ministry of Defence and it was certainly an improvement over what had previously existed in terms of co-ordination. But it had many weaknesses. Of these, the first was that it was operationally cumbersome. For example the Chief of the Defence Staff having identified a requirement which involved the participation of more than one service, had to pass his instructions to the relevant Commanders-in-Chief via service departments. It would have been more efficient for him to deal with them directly as individuals, or at least to deal with one of the Commander-in-Chief's Committees, if the operation concerned came within its mandate.

The other main weakness was that resources were allocated to the individual services on the basis of enabling them to maintain themselves in such a state as to be capable of undertaking such tasks as might be allocated to them from time to time, rather than for the purpose of carrying out certain agreed commitments. The result was that much of the discussion that went on within the Ministry of Defence, ostensibly to establish operational priorities, was distorted to suit the interests of the individual services. In a sense this was similar to the way in which representatives of the separate 'arms' in the army try to distort the deliberations of the army chain of command for the benefit of their own 'arm', but in terms of determining defence policy the results were more serious because the same people constituted the chain of command as represented the interests of the individual services, i.e. the heads of the three services, known as the Chief of the Naval Staff, the Chief of the General Staff (army) and the Chief of the Air Staff. Furthermore the importance of the issues and the scale of the resources involved was in each case far greater.

In 1982, partly as a result of the experience gained in the Falkland Islands war, the then Secretary of State for Defence decided to tackle the first of these weaknesses by placing Commanders-in-Chief directly under the Chief of the Defence Staff for operational matters. In order to strengthen the position of the Chief of the Defence Staff and the central Defence Staff over the individual service departments, he had in the previous year reallocated the duties of the ministers on a functional basis and thereby put an end to the system whereby each of the three services had their own minister. Although there was some opposition to the reallocation of duties amongst ministers, there was general support for the measures taken to improve the system of operational command which could only be regarded as long overdue. These developments took place when Sir John Nott was Secretary of State for Defence.

But despite the value of these reforms they produced a serious anomaly in that the system for allocating resources no longer matched arrangements for formulating policy and exercising command. The next Secretary for Defence, Michael Heseltine, therefore set in train a major reorganization of the Ministry of Defence designed to make the central Defence Staff responsible for the formulation of policy and the allocation of resources, thus leaving the single service departments responsible only for the management of their services. This move was greeted with a certain lack of enthusiasm and the plan arrived at for implementing it bore evidence of the compromises which had to be accepted in order to get it agreed.

Despite the resultant weaknesses, the present situation represents a great advance on that which existed before the advent of Sir John Nott and Michael Heseltine. In theory at least, resource allocation will be assessed by the central Defence Staff on the basis of commitments which concern more than one service, e.g. the 'land/air battle in the Central Region', the 'tri-service defence of the United Kingdom', 'tri-service operations outside the NATO area', etc. The business of obtaining and allocating resources in accordance with these assessments will be handled by a group composed mainly of civil servants operating under the direction of the Permanent Under Secretary of State; resource allocation being geared to the priority given to the concept concerned.

It follows that the additional resources needed to rectify the weaknesses mentioned earlier regarding the army's ability to carry out some of its commitments will only be forthcoming if the tri-service commitment, of which the army's commitment forms part, is afforded the necessary priority by the Defence Staff. This cuts both ways. On the one hand it means that the extra resources needed might be found at the expense of another service, but equally money which might formerly have gone to the army could now be diverted in order to enable another service to improve its contribution towards covering a commitment that was seen as being of a higher priority. In short it is no longer possible to get resources to offset army weaknesses by making army savings, since they could easily be used to offset a weakness in one of the other services if a higher priority was given to rectifying that.

In theory at least, that is the present system for determining policy and for allocating resources. In practice it is unlikely that it will work very well to start with, both because the reorganization of the Ministry of Defence did not go far enough and because ingrained habits of doing business will not die out overnight merely because the system has been altered. No doubt the fact that the new system has some fundamental shortcomings will be used by the people who do not want it to work as a reason for going back to the old system, although it would make more sense to eradicate the shortcomings. This should be done in two phases. The first would be to make the system as designed by Michael Heseltine more practical. The second would be to take it a stage further in order to make it more efficient.

There are two important things which need to be done to make the present system more practical. The more important is to ensure that appointments are held by the right people. Clearly if policy is to be made and resources allocated by a central Defence Staff rather than by three separate service departments,

120

then the members of the three services who have got to make the policy work, must have faith in the competence of that Defence Staff. This in turn depends on jobs being held by people who are qualified to hold them, both by virtue of their individual competence and their past training and experience. At present far too many of the influential posts are filled on a rotational basis between the services, merely to ensure that each has a fair share of the senior ranks. Even if this was the fairest system it would still be a bad one, since it would not ensure that the right man was in the right place. In fact, it is not even fair, since the strength of each of the services is so very different.

At the risk of creating a diversion from the main line of the argument, it is worth mentioning that the need to provide attractive career prospects within a service affects the way in which the Ministry of Defence is staffed since the system for staffing the Ministry of Defence with senior officers is partly based on the requirement to provide opportunities for promotion to the various grades of admiral and to a lesser extent to air marshal and general. The reason why this factor has such a bearing on the Ministry of Defence is that opportunities outside the Ministry are limited by the size of the services. In this context it is interesting to see that in 1985 the army, which was then 249,000 strong, was run by 87 general officers, i.e. full generals, lieutenant generals and major generals, whereas the 94,000 strong Air Force was run by 56 assorted air marshals and the 77,000 strong Navy by 51 assorted admirals. (In each case the strength of the services given excludes Individual Reservists but includes auxiliaries such as the Territorial Army and the Royal Navy Volunteer Reserve, because at the higher levels the problems of preparing them for war are fully integrated with those of the regular forces and make just as much work.) Although it does not necessarily follow that the ratio of senior officers to men should be the same in each service, it is at least worth noting that if it were and if the ratio of admirals to men was right, then the army should have had 208 generals instead of 87, whereas if the ratio of generals to men was right, the navy should have been able to manage on 22 admirals instead of 51.

Returning to the matter of ensuring that appointments on the central Defence Staff are held by the people best suited to discharging them, it is only necessary to add that some will always have to be occupied by a person from a particular service because only someone from that service would have the specialist knowledge required. Selection for the remainder of the senior posts must be organized on a tri-service basis by tri-service boards with access to all that is known about the candidates for the job.

The second thing that needs to be done in order to improve the chances of the new system working properly is to bring the arrangements for exercising patronage into line with it. At present although an officer on a tri-service staff may have his report written by a member of one of the other services, appointments remain in the hands of the individual services. It is high time that all appointments to the two top ranks at least (three and four star) should be made by a tri-service board consisting of the Chief of the Defence Staff, the heads of the three services and the three principal Commanders-in-Chief.

Turning to the longer term, it will ultimately be necessary to take the reorganization of the Ministry of Defence a stage further so as to eliminate the three single service departments altogether. Although the short term measures mentioned would at least make the new system workable it will still be very cumbersome because the Defence Staff's responsibility for establishing policy, allocating resources and exercising operational command overlaps with the service departments' responsibility for managing their individual services. Thus it is bound to happen that a Commander-in-Chief will become involved in lengthy exchanges with the Defence Staff in order to get some matter sorted out, only to find at the end of the day that he has to go back to his own service department and go through the whole business again in order to convince a different collection of individuals who have a different viewpoint of the merits of his case.

In practice there would be no difficulty in tacking the component parts of the service departments on to the relevant sections of the Defence Staff. For example, there is a part of the Defence Staff which deals with personnel and it would be easy enough for the three single service personnel branches to be added to it. Obviously, for the reasons given earlier, that part of the Defence Staff which dealt with army personnel would have to be staffed by army officers and the same would apply to the other two services, but matters common to the men and women of all three services could be dealt with by a tri-service part of the staff. There is nothing very revolutionary in this proposal, which is exactly how the business of procuring weapons and equipment for all three services has been managed for some years. The same considerations apply equally to logistics.

In practice the main difficulty in streamlining the Ministry of Defence comes from trying to safeguard the position of the heads of the three services. Ideally at the time of the reorganization the roles of these people should have been changed so as to make them the Chief of the Defence Staff's principal advisers on their services whilst continuing to form the Chiefs of Staff's Committee. In that capacity they would have been looked after by the Defence Staff and would have needed no separate staff of their own. As part of the Defence Staff they would have been able to retain the full range of their influence on formulating defence policy and on the allocation of resources and they could even have been used on occasions by the Chief of the Defence Staff to deal with Commanders-in-Chief on his behalf on operational matters.

Presumably this did not happen because the constitutional adjustments, and the additional fuss that would have ensued from appearing to weaken the position of the heads of the three services, were more than the Secretary of State could manage politically. In practice, by placing them outside the real seat of power, the present arrangement will leave the heads with less influence than they would have had if the alteration had been made, notwithstanding the number of staff officers who remain working for them.

Although it is of great importance that the Ministry of Defence is properly organized, organization cannot of itself overcome the problems which bedevil attempts at providing the resources necessary for securing the defence interests of the United

Kingdom. Of these problems, the two most difficult to resolve are the fixing of defence priorities and coping with the escalating cost of equipment.

Clearly there would be little difficulty in fixing defence priorities if it were possible to forecast exactly what was going to happen. For example, if it was certain that the only sort of major war that was likely to develop was a Russian attack on NATO which lasted for about ten days before a ceasefire was arranged then it is clear what would be required of the three services. In this case top priority would have to be given to the allocation of resources required for fighting the land/air battle in Europe, with a smaller amount being diverted to securing the defence of the United Kingdom for a limited period and keeping open a sea/air corridor across the Atlantic to the extent necessary for passing over first echelon reinforcements from the United States. The same resources for the most part could be considered available for use outside the NATO area in peacetime and the only extra of any significance would be resources allocated to the provision of an independent nuclear deterrent designed to give a little extra confidence to any of the European members of the alliance who might be worrying about how far the Americans would be prepared to go in defence of Europe. That is more or less the situation which prevailed during the 1970s.

But the fact that the door in the Central Region of Europe is now so well barred means that an attack there is unlikely to take place, providing of course that the defences in central Europe are not weakened. Having said that, it is difficult to forecast what will happen, although a number of different situations could arise. These could include a less direct attack on NATO such as a limited movement on one of the extremities, or possibly even at sea, carried out in such a way as to make it unlikely to provoke a nuclear response, whilst at the same time making it difficult to counter while NATO forces are so heavily geared to fighting a battle in the Central Region. Alternatively there might be a threat to a sensitive place outside the NATO area or the fostering of insurgency in a friendly country, etc. The difficulty lies in the fact that there are insufficient resources available to be strong everywhere and by the very act of becoming strong in one direction the danger switches elsewhere.

The current defence policy of the United Kingdom represents an attempt to contribute towards the composite requirements of the NATO alliance whilst keeping a bit extra for private British needs plus an element of insurance against a change in the circumstances which led to the formulation of the composite NATO requirements in the first place. The difficulty is that a change in the world balance of nuclear weapons and an improvement in the anti-tank capability of NATO means that the Central Region threat is not nearly so likely to develop as some of the others. This in turn means that much more needs to be spent on countering some of the other threats, but, at the same time, no less can be spent on the Central Region without increasing the danger there. In other words, more resources are needed in a number of areas without it being possible to save much in any area. None the less it would be difficult to get the British taxpayer to provide significant extra resources, especially as he already does more for defence than his counterparts in most of the countries of the alliance.

But if nothing is done, either to get more resources or to save on current commitments, the defences of the United Kingdom will become progressively less effective despite the considerable sacrifices of the British taxpayer. The nettle must be grasped, which means that priorities must be adjusted to the changes which are taking place. In theory at least there are plenty of alternative ways in which this can be done, although most of them would involve a lot of hard bargaining with allies, and one of the difficulties lies in getting some of them to understand that safeguarding places far removed from their own borders is often as important to them as it is to the United Kingdom.

The most frequently expressed suggestion for providing the extra resources required is to do away with the independent British strategic nuclear capability and to use the money on extra conventional forces so as to improve coverage of other commitments. It could be argued that up to the middle of the 1970s it would have been possible for the United Kingdom to do without an independent nuclear capability, because the very close identity of interest with America and the total predominance of

America within the NATO alliance meant that her overwhelming nuclear superiority provided sufficient nuclear cover for all the allies. During this period America's nuclear capability made sense of the conventional armaments of all the NATO countries in the context discussed in Chapter 1.

But with the gradual erosion of her nuclear superiority and the increasing divergence of interest which is becoming apparent between America on the one hand and some of the European members of NATO on the other, it is no longer sensible to suppose that America's nuclear capability could always be counted on to balance each individual NATO country's conventional forces, especially in terms of disputes which might arise outside the NATO context. This will become even more relevant as additional countries throughout the world become nuclear powers. It is not only a case of worrying about whether America would abandon her European allies in an acute crisis in order to save her own people. It is as much a case of some European members of NATO wanting to go their own way at the expense of helping America when a crisis occurs which America thinks to be of fundamental importance to her interests. If the United Kingdom ever wishes to be able to act independently of America, or even to opt out of following America on certain occasions, she must have an independent nuclear capability which is genuinely able to deter any hostile power.

This has only recently become practicable because the development of weapons as powerful as Trident enables medium sized powers, such as Britain or France, to pose an effective deterrent to a superpower such as Russia now, or possibly some other country in the future. But it is no good having second rate nuclear weapons for this purpose. Only weapons capable of penetrating the defences of any potential enemy will do.

Another aspect of this problem relates to the position of West Germany. If West Germany should ever want to follow an independent line to that of America, it will face the same problem as the United Kingdom or France. But it hardly has the same options, since it would be virtually impossible for it to have its own independent nuclear capability without getting Russia so agitated as to upset any hope of world peace, let alone of long term multilateral disarmament. This is not primarily because of the Russian recollection of events long passed, but because of the more immediate problems of a split Germany today. If the West Germans ever feel the need to be truly independent of America they must be able to get nuclear cover from another ally, should the need arise. If this proves impossible, the only other alternative would be to exchange NATO membership for some form of neutrality as mentioned in Chapter 2. The United Kingdom and France, or possibly just one of them, might be able to provide enough reassurance to Germany to enable it to retain its position in the Western camp, provided that they possessed a sufficiently effective nuclear capability.

Thus, regardless of whether the United Kingdom has needed its own nuclear capability over the past forty years, it will certainly need it in the future, and it needs a very effective one. Without it, much of the money spent on other aspects of defence will be money wasted. Luckily it is one of the most economic forms of military power available, despite the efforts of some commentators to indicate the contrary by quoting expenditure figures for the one or two years when they are at their highest because of the changeover between Polaris and Trident. Only by looking at them in the long term can they be compared sensibly with other defence capabilities.

Although it would be wrong, for reasons already discussed, to suppose that the possession of nuclear weapons makes other forms of defence unnecessary, it is none the less true to say that an independent and effective nuclear capability is essential to the United Kingdom. Neither dismantling it nor failing to renew it is, therefore, a practical way of providing the extra resources needed. This is unfortunate as much of the argument for retention could be used by other countries to justify their need for nuclear weapons and people are rightly concerned at the thought of proliferation. But if a country believes it to be in its interests to possess nuclear weapons and if it can afford them and cannot be prevented by outside pressure from having them, then it will obtain them regardless of whether the United Kingdom possesses them or not.

Apart from operational priorities, the other major problem concerning the provision of resources is that the cost of weapons and equipment escalates faster than the rate of inflation so that an ever greater proportion of the defence budget has to be spent on procuring them at the expense of other more important matters such as training and personnel. To some extent this fact is due to the increasing complexity of modern technology but there are at least two other causes of cost escalation which could be controlled if the necessary incentive existed.

The first of these is the natural desire always to have the best. Most weapons or new equipments take many years to develop and produce, and throughout the period new technology is providing new opportunities. Thus the user is constantly being told that if he is prepared to wait a few months longer and pay a few thousand (or million) pounds more, he can have something that is very much better. It is natural to want to do this, especially if intelligence sources are making the point that the equipment as originally ordered will only be effective for a very limited period in the light of what is known of new equipment coming into service with the potential enemy. Certainly on some occasions it is right to wait a bit longer and pay a bit more, but on many others it is more sensible to accept what was originally ordered, provided that it will meet the need, even if something more expensive might do the job better.

The second case is far more complex. Much of the cost of a piece of equipment comes from paying for the research required and for the practical experimenting that has to be done in order to turn this research into a workable weapon or piece of equipment. If an American or European equipment can be found which meets the requirement it may be cheaper to buy this off the peg than to develop a suitable piece of equipment within the country. It would, however, pay to develop it domestically if enough can be sold to overseas buyers to cover the research and production costs. If equipment is developed which is in great demand abroad it may even make a big profit. So even in terms of the cost of research and development, it is not necessarily more economic to buy abroad.

There are two other factors that have to be taken into account.

128

The first is the danger of buying abroad should the seller decide for some reason to stop the supply, or to cease supplying spares at a difficult moment when no alternative could be found. It could happen that the seller was forced by circumstances to cease the supply totally against his will, e.g. if his factories were destroyed or if it became impossible to move the stuff. There is therefore an element of risk in relying on an overseas supplier.

The other factor relates to the loss of employment within British scientific laboratories and factories which comes from buying abroad. At the best of times there is a certain reluctance on the part of the public to pay for defence, a reluctance which would be intensified if jobs were lost by buying more equipments overseas: and there is no doubt that a very large number of jobs within the United Kingdom are dependent on the needs of defence. There is one other point to be made which is that there is nothing more likely to bring about escalating costs than to let one firm gain a monopoly in any particular area of defence expenditure, particularly if it is government owned.

In summing up the matter of escalation in the costs of weapons and equipment it is only necessary to make the following points. First, the possibility of buying abroad should be examined in every case where it is unlikely that overseas sales will result in home produced equipment being sold at an overall profit. Second, no weapon or equipment or range of equipments should be developed domestically if there is not a long term future for it, since the development costs of one generation of weapons are often not recovered in terms of overseas sales until the second or third generation is produced and sold. Third, vulnerability in terms of buying abroad is a legitimate defence consideration but loss of jobs is not: if the government wants to use taxpayers' money to safeguard employment it does not need to pass it through the defence vote. In any case there are other ways of safeguarding employment in the defence industries without paying for research and development costs: for example, equipment developed overseas can be manufactured on licence in the United Kingdom. There is also a good compromise position whereby research and development costs are shared by entering into collaborative projects with one or more

129

other countries. This is particularly relevant to another issue, i.e. the business of strengthening the hand of European countries *vis-à-vis* America.

But even if all these precautions are taken in the firmest possible manner, there is no doubt that equipment costs will continue to escalate so that either the country will have to pay more proportionately for defence than it does now, or it will have to adjust its commitments.

It is now possible to return to the question of finding resources with which to rectify shortcomings in the army's ability to meet its commitments and in this connection three things are plain to see. First, although a lot of the mayhem caused by the escalating cost of weapons and equipment could be avoided if the political will for doing so existed, there is no scope for saving enough money by this means to put right the army's shortcomings. The best that can be hoped for is to reduce the rate of escalation. Second, it is no good trying to juggle with the priorities of army commitments in isolation in order to provide the necessary resources to enable some of them to be carried out successfully at the expense of others: it is only possible to readjust priorities on a tri-service basis. Third, it is absolutely necessary to make a major reassessment of tri-service defence commitments within the next few years since if a lot of resources are not saved in this way that can be used to rectify shortcomings, the army will eventually become ineffective and the same can probably be said for the other two services as well.

Although it is beyond the scope of this book and the competence of the author to make a detailed analysis of tri-service commitments worldwide one point is clear, which is that nuclear weapons are relatively cheap and highly effective in terms of promoting Britain's defence interests for the reasons mentioned earlier in this chapter, and should certainly be retained. If all other British defence capabilities were represented by the blades of a pair of scissors, the nuclear capability would be the bolt that holds the blades together and enables them to cut.

For the rest, as a detailed analysis is not possible, an example will be given of the sort of adjustment that could be made which might be workable and at the same time sufficiently sweeping to provide the scale of resources needed. It is based on a major change being made to an army commitment which would not only save resources, but also put an end to the division which exists in the army as a result of the units which are stationed in Germany having to specialize to so great an extent on armoured and mechanized warfare.

This could be achieved by the British Army withdrawing altogether from the Central Region of NATO and taking over instead, the responsibility for defending West Germany north of the River Elbe, i.e. Hamburg and Schleswig-Holstein. It would involve moving the British Corps from their present camps and barracks in Westphalia and Lower Saxony and installing them in Schleswig-Holstein. At the same time the German troops already there would move to cover the gap in the Central Region and the Danish troops now earmarked to assist in the defence of this area would be used in Zealand, thus removing the need for the British to reinforce that place.

As mentioned earlier, the length of front which the British Corps would have to cover would not be greatly different and all the 55,000 troops now stationed in Germany would still be required in the new position. There would be no question whatsoever of fewer British soldiers being stationed in Germany in peacetime. But the terrain in the new area is different and more suited to defence, so that the composition of the force and the tactics employed would be different and more compatible with other army commitments. An important part of the arrangement would be that as the British Corps might require a smaller number of armoured and mechanized forces than is the case in the Central Region, the reduced number of tanks and armoured personnel carriers that would be needed could perhaps be bought from the Germans and the whole of the research and development costs of this sort of war could be saved. Furthermore, the depth of the country from front to rear is less, so that fewer reinforcing units would be needed to safeguard the rear areas and man the lines of communication. An additional advantage would be that the British would be defending a part of Germany that was of

131

vital importance to them and they would be doing it by themselves, so they could not afford to take any risks based on the idea that the Germans would bail them out if things went wrong.

From the point of view of NATO's Northern Region, the proposal would lead to a tidier and more efficient system, with the Danish army concentrated in the place that is most important to them from a political point of view, i.e. Zealand. There would be very little disruption of the current command arrangements; all that would happen is that the command in Schleswig-Holstein (now exercised by an officer known as COM-LANDJUT) would cease to rotate between the Germans and the Danes and would be taken over by the commander of the British Corps. The office of Commander Baltic Approaches (COM-BALTAP) would remain in Danish hands and that of Commander-in-Chief Allied Forces Northern Region in British hands. There would, however, have to be a considerable reshuffle of the air force contribution to the Region, but that is long overdue in any case because of a confused air boundary which exists between the Northern and Central Regions.

From the point of view of NATO's Central Region, the matter is more complicated because the present German contribution to the defence of Schleswig-Holstein is smaller than the British Corps whose positions they would have to take over in the Central Region. They would therefore find difficulty in plugging the gap. But there would be many advantages from the German point of view. First, it would mean that there would be one less nation involved in the northern part of the Central Region which would be a help in terms of the standardization of equipment used, with all that is entailed in rationalizing logistics. Furthermore, German forces would outnumber the other nationalities, especially if their territorial forces are taken into account, and they could therefore claim the tactically influential appointment of Commander Northern Army Group, which is important for them if the battle is to be fought on an army group basis as opposed to a series of vaguely co-ordinated corps battles. Few officers other than the Germans have the military education and background to think in this way.

Other advantages which might accrue to the Germans would be that they could probably pick up the overseas sales of weapons relating to armoured and mechanized warfare that the British would lose by opting out of research and development in this field. Another advantage of a different sort would be that Hamburg and Schleswig-Holstein would be better defended than under the present arrangements and the same might even be said of the West German Plain since such troops as would be there would at least start from much nearer to their battle positions: there would be no need to rely on reinforcements arriving from England. As stated in Chapter 2 this is one of the major weaknesses of the present plan.

One major advantage from the British point of view would be the saving that would result from abandoning the cost of researching and developing weapons and equipment suitable for armoured warfare and also from having to buy less of them: this is one of the main expenses of the army overall. This saving could in fact be made without switching the British contribution from the Central Region to Schleswig-Holstein but it would be less easy to accept whilst the armoured and mechanized content of the force was so overwhelmingly important.

There would be many other advantages. For example it would not be necessary to send so many reinforcements to bolster the 55,000 men stationed in Schleswig-Holstein in peace. By combining the most effective parts of the reinforcing formations which are at present held to cover the requirements of both the Northern and Central Regions (excluding the UK/Netherlands Amphibious Force which is in any case earmarked for NATO's Atlantic Command) it should be possible to cover most of the requirement with regular troops, with some Territorial Army units being used for rear area security and some logistic units. This would greatly increase the number of Territorial Army units available for the defence of the United Kingdom as well as enabling the troops in Schleswig-Holstein to be reinforced more quickly.

By retaining one of the regular brigades now earmarked for the reinforcement of NATO in the United Kingdom and by grouping it with the one currently earmarked for use as the

133

Commander-in-Chief's reserve together with one or two Territorial Army brigades, a good sized division of mobile troops could be held ready to handle emergencies in the United Kingdom. It might also be possible in the course of reconstructing the peacetime garrison of Germany to retain some extra regular logistic units in the United Kingdom which would also strengthen the country's ability to react to events outside the NATO area in peacetime.

There would, also, be major disadvantages to making the change. For one thing the capital cost of the move would be considerable because all the barracks, married quarters and other assets which the army now has in Lower Saxony and North Rhine Westphalia, would have to be replaced by similar facilities north of the Elbe. The thought of undertaking such an exercise might not be welcomed by the civil servants in the Ministry of Defence and the Treasury. At the same time politicians of both parties would object to the loss of jobs in the defence industries and they might even try to cream off the savings made in order to reduce the defence budget rather than use the resources for rectifying existing shortcomings. There would certainly be opposition from within the army led by the 'arms' and 'services' which would lose most from shifting the emphasis away from armoured and mechanized warfare. Above all it might not be possible to persuade the Germans of the advantages of the arrangement, in which case it would be a total waste of time proceeding further because, as stated previously, one of the principal reasons for keeping British troops in Germany at all is to reassure them and keep them within the alliance.

In practice the proposal cannot be regarded as a basis for negotiation in its present form. Before this could happen a careful study would have to take place in order to ascertain the number and type of units that would be needed to defend Germany north of the Elbe and a plan would have to be made to show what part of the force would have to be stationed in the area in peace and what extra would be needed as reinforcements together with the timing involved. This is beyond the scope of a book because much of the assessment would carry a security classification which would prevent it from being published. But the purpose of putting the idea forward is to give an example of the scale of reorganization needed in order to match Britain's defence policy to the available resources. It cannot be said too often that matters must not be allowed to drift. Some really hard decisions must be taken to prevent the army from becoming incapable of carrying out its commitments as a result of a shortage of resources. The proposal given not only illustrates the scale of the reorganization required, but it also shows how many of the deep-seated divisions and anomalies within the army could be ironed out.

Chapter 9

ORGANIZATION, TRAINING
AND EQUIPMENT

Having discussed the problem of how extra resources might be made available, it is now time to see what alterations need to be made to the army in order to rectify the shortcomings in its ability to meet its commitments as described earlier. This will be covered in two chapters. The first examines in outline the changes that are needed in the way in which the army is organized, equipped, and trained. The second discusses the problems involved in making sure that the army is correctly manned. In both chapters the subject will be looked at purely in terms of how the army needs to change. No attempt is made to analyse how it works in areas where no change is necessary.

The first subject to be considered then, is organization. At the moment the internal organization of the units and formations of the field army, i.e. the formations and units that have to be ready to fight a war, is consistent with current tactical thinking, which is itself based on the weapons and equipment now in service, so there is no call for any radical change in this direction. The subjects that merit examination are first the top direction of the army, second the command structure of the field army, third the command structure of the individual training organization and base logistic units and fourth the regimental system.

Mention has already been made of the fact that advantages would accrue from merging the individual service departments in the Ministry of Defence with the central Defence Staff. This would have a bearing on the way in which the army is organized, although the organization of the Ministry of Defence is not strictly speaking an army matter. There would be two main advantages to doing this. First, it would assist Commanders-in-Chief and their staffs by doing away with the time wasting business of dealing separately with the Defence Staff on the one hand and the Army Department on the other. Second, it would remove a considerable number of senior staff posts, thus saving valuable defence resources, as well as speeding up and improving the way in which business is done.

In the long term it may prove desirable to replace the Commanders-in-Chief's Committees with single tri-service Commanders-in-Chief, thereby pushing down one level further the top tier of single service direction. But this should not be attempted until the members of the individual services discover that genuine tri-service direction from the Ministry of Defence can operate objectively, that is to say until people realize that decisions are being taken in the best interests of defence rather than for the benefit of a particular service. Before tri-service Commanders-in-Chief can be introduced, the present system has got to be improved along the lines mentioned previously and the single service departments will have to be merged with the Defence Staff. Meanwhile the Commanders-in-Chief's Committees operate well enough, especially as plans exist to enable one Commander-in-Chief to command a specific operation on behalf of the Committee as a whole if desired, with the other members sending senior representatives to his headquarters to act as his deputies.

Below the Commander-in-Chief there has to be a clear chain of command within the field army in peacetime and it is essential that this should not be confused or short circuited. Three levels of command are needed between the Commander-in-Chief and the units. At the top is the army commander in the United Kingdom and the corps commander in Germany: these officers are lieutenant-generals. Below them are the district or divisional commanders, most of whom are major-generals and below them are the brigade commanders.

The reason why it is so important in peacetime to have a single clear chain of command within the field army is that if it does not exist, field army units will not be properly prepared for their operational tasks. There are two aspects to preparing

137

troops for war. The first is to find out what is required of them, and the second is to ensure that they are organized, trained and equipped to carry out the particular tasks that are likely to come their way. Neither of these functions will be carried out correctly unless a proper chain of command exists with commanders at the various levels collecting the appropriate data, making effective plans and seeing that they are put into effect. In order to justify the claim that three levels are needed between the units and the Commanders-in-Chief the task at each level must be examined.

Immediately above the unit comes the brigade commander and all units need a superior commander at this level who can be responsible for the supervision and support of the commanding officers. It is the brigadier who can get to know personalities, who can assess weaknesses and who can take the necessary action to rectify them. The number of units which one brigadier can command in peace must be related to the distances he will have to travel and the means of transport available to him. It is important that officers filling these appointments should have the right background experience in relation to the tasks for which their units are being prepared and be of the right age in relation to the commanding officers of the units and the subordinate commanders within the units. It is a happy thought that at the time of writing virtually all units are in brigades, although not all the brigadiers are as well qualified in terms of age and experience as they might be. No organizational change is therefore called for at the moment and therefore, strictly speaking, the inclusion of the last three paragraphs is not justified by the stated purpose of this chapter.

But it is vital to stress the importance of ensuring that the present situation is not eroded, because the removal of the brigade level of command is a method of making economies which is tempting to senior army officers trying to ensure that savings forced upon them do not take the form of the disbandment of old established regiments. This is both understandable and commendable in itself but it leaves two things out of account. The first is that the regiments saved thereby and all the others as well, will be rendered ineffective if they are not properly directed

138

from above. The second is that there are many other ways of making savings that would be far less injurious such as the absorption of the Army Department by the Defence Staff or the destruction of the headquarters of the various 'arms' and 'services'. Another point to bear in mind is that the existence of units is not something that should be threatened by the need to make savings: it must be related to the number required to meet the army's commitments. If a major commitment is cut and the long term need for one or more units is clearly seen to have disappeared, then it is reasonable that disbandments should take place. But if this is not the case, then disbandment of units should not be seen as a method of making savings.

Reverting to the chain of command in the field army, all the brigade commanders should themselves be subordinate to major-generals commanding districts or divisions and whose job is totally different. Their job is to ensure that an adequate link is maintained with the formation who will be using the brigades, or the units within the brigades, in war, if different from the peacetime arrangement: this is usually the case because so many units move on the outbreak of war to formations other than those which look after them in peace. By maintaining this link, major-generals can ensure that the brigade commanders are training their units against clearly defined operational concepts which are realistic in terms of the capabilities of the units. If each individual brigade commander tried to maintain this link for himself, he would become involved in a vast amount of extra travelling and would not have time to visit his units. The major-generals are also responsible for training and testing the brigade commanders so that they too are capable of carrying out their wartime roles. In addition planning and allocating resources for training and monitoring the organization and equipment of the units is their responsibility. Such tasks could not be undertaken by the brigade commanders unless they had much larger staffs than they need to carry out their present functions, and in any case they could not exercise and test themselves. It is an undoubted fact that in the past far too many unit and brigade commanders have been promoted without being properly tested.

The peacetime job of the commander of the field army in the United Kingdom and the corps commander in Germany is the co-ordination of the long term training plan and the allocation of resources. They are also concerned with keeping operational concepts under review in order to ensure that the way in which formations are organized, trained and equipped reflects the changes in the tactical plans and thinking of the commanders who will be using their formations in war. It is therefore the lieutenant-generals who are responsible for most of the top level contacts with the NATO commanders in Europe and with American commanders with whom British forces might find themselves fighting outside the NATO area.

In wartime a clear chain of command is also required at distinct and separate levels but it may not be at the same levels as in peacetime. In a major theatre of operations, such as the Central Region of NATO, the three levels of corps, division and brigade are certainly needed: commanders at each level have their own job to do and each is thinking and planning for a different time ahead. It is a certain recipe for disaster to muddle up their responsibilities. But in other theatres of operation the same three levels may not be needed. For example, in a counter-insurgency campaign the important thing is to match the chain of command to the levels at which the civil government is working. In an operation that might be taking place outside the NATO area the command chain would have to be tailored to suit the size and circumstances of the operation. For example in the Falkland Islands war there was no three-star (lieutenant-general) level of command between the Commander-in-Chief and the major-general commanding the ground forces or the rear-admiral at sea in the South Atlantic, although the Commander-in-Chief did have naval and air deputies of three-star rank in his headquarters in England.

There can be little doubt that it is expensive to maintain the right number of senior commanders within the field army, but that is what generals and brigadiers are for. The problem arises from the pressures which always exist to increase the number of brigadiers and generals in other parts of the army such as the Ministry of Defence, the higher headquarters and in the static organizations that carry out individual training and administrative functions. The reasons for this are complex, but they include the desire to produce balanced career prospects in those regiments and corps that do not usually produce commanders in the field army, the desire to employ officers long after they have ceased to be of any use as commanders in the field and the desire on the part of civil servants to have plenty of senior service officers in the Ministry of Defence to justify a similarly inflated establishment of their own. Unfortunately ministers, who are the only people capable of opposing these pressures, are usually content to say that they don't mind where senior officers are employed, providing that there are not more than a certain number of them. But despite the problems, unless the field army is properly commanded by men with the right experience and of the right age, it will not withstand the impact of war. Nothing else is of comparable importance. In the nuclear age there will be no period of grace to sort things out after the war starts, which is the traditional British way of doing business.

Having looked at the way the field army is organized, the next thing is to examine briefly how the individual training organization and the base administrative units are commanded. At the head of the individual training organization there is a lieutenant-general who is comparable in command terms with the commander of the field army or the corps commander in Germany. He commands all the establishments in the individual training organization such as the Staff College or the Arms Schools or the training depots. Some of these establishments are themselves commanded by major-generals or brigadiers although most are commanded by lieutenant colonels. As there are about ninety of them, excluding the very small ones, it would be impossible for the lieutenant-general to command all of them directly, so there is a rather messy intermediate level composed of the heads of each of the 'arms' and 'services', who give instructions to the commanders of the various establishments as to how the training in them should be carried out, and the district commanders who are responsible for their administration. From a training point of view the business would be carried out better if the heads of the various 'arms' and 'services' were abolished and

141

the whole responsibility given to the district commanders. Both the lieutenant-general and the district commanders would need an increase in their staffs to cope with the extra work, but this would be more than offset by the savings made by disposing of all the 'arms' and 'service' headquarters.

Unfortunately there are other considerations involved. First, as described in Chapter 6, the headquarters of each of the 'arms' and 'services' are also involved in formulating views on matters such as tactics, weapons and procedures, related to their 'arms' and 'services' with which to lobby the chain of command. Although this is neither necessary nor desirable, since the commanders in the chain of command can get all the special advice they need either from their own staffs or by asking the commanders of their own 'arms' or 'service' units, it is a traditional way of doing business. Another problem with regard to disbanding the headquarters of the logistic services is that they are used as agents by the Army Department in the Ministry of Defence to command the base logistic units in the United Kingdom. Again this is totally unnecessary, since it could equally well be handled by the headquarters of United Kingdom Land Forces through the district headquarters like all the other units stationed in the United Kingdom. The only reason why the present system is retained is that it provides a justification for maintaining a logistic staff in the Army Department, separate to the logistic part of the central Defence Staff. It also supports the case for retaining a considerable number of extra senior officers since colonels and brigadiers are used in the Ministry of Defence to do jobs that are done by captains and majors in a district headquarters or in the headquarters of United Kingdom Land Forces.

Although this description of the way matters are arranged outside the field army is rather too detailed by comparison with the importance of the subject, it is entirely relevant to the problem of finding enough senior officers to command the field army properly. It is also closely connected with the allocation of resources since whenever economies are needed, the pressure which is brought to bear in order to save this vast edifice of unwanted senior officers inevitably results in the disestablishment of something useful in the logistic or administrative field

142

such as a section of military policemen or part of a workshop.

In case it should be thought that the situation is being exaggerated the following example of the British Army's propensity for employing senior officers is given. For every major-general and above in the German army once it is fully mobilized, there would be 25,000 troops. The figure in the American army would be 13,000, in the Dutch army 12,400, in the Norwegian army 11,200, in the Danish army 9,000, in the Belgian army 8,800, and in the French army 8,200. In the British Army it would be 4,500. It could be argued that these figures are unfair, because all the other countries mentioned have more numerous reserves than the British. But if full-time soldiers are taken as the criteria, the result is not far different. In this case the order would be Germany with one general to 8,800 men followed by France, Holland, America and Belgium in that order. Britain would come next, bracketed with the Danes, with one general to every 1,800 men, the Norwegians being slightly more extravagant with one general to 1,200 men. The only way to make the British figure seem reasonably respectable is to count the Territorial Army in the full-time figures. This is perfectly fair in terms of the work caused by the Territorial Army, but unfair as a basis for comparison with other armies because no other country has anything comparable to it. If, however, this is done, the British would come half-way down the league, below Germany, France, Holland and America but above Belgium, Denmark and Norway.[1] However, when looking at the proportion of generals to troops, it should be remembered that at least the army is more economic than the other two services.

Reverting to the command structure of the British Army, what is needed is a proper chain of command manned by commanders and staff officers who are adequately qualified and of the right rank to do the job and no more. Any additional resources should be used on things which increase the army's ability to carry out its commitments. It is also important that commanders and staff officers should be left in their jobs for long enough to assess what is going on, to decide whether alterations are needed and to put these into effect. The reason why the army so often fails to make alterations in time, is not, as

143

a rule, because army officers are conservative in their thinking. More often it is because they are not left in a job for long enough to make the necessary reforms. The more complex the job, the longer it should be held by the same person. A series of radical and energetic officers relieving each other in an appointment at short intervals will achieve less than one sensible person who remains in the post for a longer period.

The last organizational matter which merits consideration is the regimental system. It has already been pointed out that this constitutes the greatest strength of the British Army because it is one of the main reasons why the soldiers on the ground behave so well when the going gets rough, and nothing is more important than that. But the regimental system is an expression covering a variety of different arrangements which have little in common except that they are all designed to foster the feeling of belonging to a group that will hold together against outside pressure. The fact that the arrangements differ is partly because the groups have different needs, but it is also due to the way events have unfolded over the years and it is by no means true to say that each manifestation of the regimental system is as good as the next. As the regimental system is not the most economic way of organizing the army, it is important to make it work as well as possible, in order to ensure that it is not vulnerable to attack by those who measure everything in terms of cost accounting. There has been plenty of criticism of the regimental system in the past and there is bound to be more in the future.

When covering the way in which the army is organized in Chapter 6, it was explained that the regimental system was originally designed for the infantry and the cavalry, but that it was subsequently extended in a modified form to cover the needs of the other 'arms' and the logistic and administrative 'services'. There is no need to go further into the way in which the system works in its modified form, because in each case the regiment or its equivalent corps, e.g. the corps of Royal Engineers, is a large enough group for there to be few uneconomic overheads and the work which they do is sufficiently different to that of the infantry and the armoured corps (descendants of the cavalry) for the closeness of the family group to be of less importance. Discussion will therefore be limited to the infantry and the armoured corps.

Although so far as the infantry is concerned the regimental system originated in the middle of the seventeenth century, it was more than two centuries later, as part of the Cardwell reforms, that it took a form that is recognizable today. It was at that time that regiments were recruited from a specific geographical area such as a county and divided into two battalions; one to be stationed in the United Kingdom and the other overseas, usually in India. The idea was that the regiment would still be a small enough entity to feel like a family, but that by having two battalions there would be scope for people to be posted between them in order to take account of promotion opportunities and to give some preference to whether a person wished to be at home or abroad. At the same time the regimental depot would enable the two battalions to pool overheads in terms of training recruits and to keep in touch with the geographical area from which the recruits were drawn. There were a few exceptions to the grounding of regiments in specific geographical areas, notably the foot guards and the rifle regiments.

The Cardwell system was practical, efficient and adaptable. It even worked after a fashion during two world wars when more and more battalions were added to existing regiments, but there was obviously a dilution of the family feeling which then tended to become focused on the particular battalion rather than on the regiment as a whole. Furthermore, the major disasters that took place from time to time meant that battalions that got decimated were often built up with reinforcements from other regiments. All of this was inevitable, but it had its effect and there are some authorities who would maintain that the quality of the infantry deteriorated considerably as the world wars progressed, particularly in the Second World War. It is hardly surprising that the system creaked a bit under the impact, since no one had ever imagined war being conducted on such a scale over so long a period when it was devised. Cardwell's regimental system was excellent for preparing troops for war and was well suited to the relatively small scale limited wars that the British Army normally expected to undertake.

145

It would have been perfectly possible for the army to have reverted to this practical system after the Second World War as it did after the first, but a new factor intervened in that immediately after the war ended, the British left India. As a result, and despite the need to keep some battalions in Germany, the overall number of battalions required in the British Army in peacetime diminished. This situation could have been handled by disbanding regiments of two battalions and retaining other regiments of two battalions until the right number was reached. But the decision as to which regiments to keep and which to disband was too painful and the easy way out was taken which merely involved disbanding each regiment's second battalion. The result was a partial reversion to the situation which existed before Cardwell with all the problems arising from the fact that the regimental family was too small. Overheads were no longer being shared in the same way and the opportunities provided by moving people from one battalion to another in the same regiment were lost. The whole system rapidly became less efficient, less economic and open to criticism. It was at this time that demands were made for the infantry to be organized into a large corps like, for example, the Royal Engineers.

The next thing that happened was that the gradual withdrawal from the remainder of the Empire started to gain momentum and further reductions in the number of infantry battalions were found to be necessary. But now there were no easy options left, as the regiments were all down to one battalion anyway. The right answer would have been a major reconstruction of the infantry by amalgamating pairs of regiments, so that each new regiment had two battalions, or better still to amalgamate three regiments into one new one of three battalions, since that would still have been small enough for the family feeling to exist and would have left scope for further reduction later to a viable two battalion regiment.

Something like this was attempted but many of the regiments made such a fuss that looser groupings were permitted. As a result, some individual one battalion regiments were allowed to retain their identity whilst being grouped with a number of others for the sharing of overheads and the interposting of individuals. Others were disbanded altogether. This system has now been further refined and institutionalized within what are known as divisions of infantry (not to be confused with the field army formation also known as a division which is a grouping of brigades). Each division of infantry consists of a number of regiments who share the overheads of a depot for the training of recruits. In some of these divisions there are two or three regiments of three battalions each, formed by amalgamations in the post-war period, and they function fully as regiments in their own right. Other divisions consist of eight or nine single battalion regiments which can only function effectively by posting people to and from each other. They are in effect battalions of a very large regiment which is their parent division of infantry and this particular variation represents an erosion of the regimental system: it is also less flexible than the other version. For example, if it were desired to lengthen the time a battalion was to stay in a particular theatre, such as Germany, in order to reduce the costs of movement and to get the unit better trained in the mechanized role, it would be easy to do in a three battalion regiment, because individuals could be moved from one battalion to another without leaving the regiment. But in the case of the single battalion regiments all the postings necessary would have to be outside the regiment.

The regimental system must also be viewed in the the context of the Territorial Army. There are broadly speaking three main variations of it in use within the infantry of the Territorial Army. First, there are regiments consisting of two or three battalions which are not directly linked to regiments of the regular army. Examples in this category are the Highland Volunteers, the Lowland Volunteers, the Yorkshire Volunteers and the Wessex Regiment. These regiments co-ordinate matters between their battalions sufficiently well to enable them to exchange officers where necessary or to take a company commander from one to become the commanding officer of another. Each of these regiments is sponsored by one of the divisions of infantry which provides the regular instructors and administrative staff.

Second, there are Territorial battalions of regular regiments which themselves have three battalions. Thus the Royal Anglian Regiment which has three regular battalions also has two Territorial battalions. In this case the regular part of the Royal Anglian Regiment, rather than a division of infantry, will provide the necessary support for the Territorial battalions, and the Royal Anglian regimental headquarters will be able to co-ordinate matters between all the battalions.

Third, there is the single battalion Territorial regiment attached to a single battalion regular regiment. In this case the single battalion regular regiment is probably too small to provide all the regular support that the Territorial battalion needs, so the parent division of infantry helps out. On the other hand, if there is only one Territorial battalion it is not possible to move people from one to another as the occasion demands and this system is definitely inferior to the other two in terms of efficiency.

But all these systems work after a fashion and there is no doubt that the men serving in the battalions are intensely proud of their regiments, regardless of the category to which they belong. Sometimes there is pressure to break up those regiments which are not tied to regular regiments, in order to provide Territorial battalions for single battalion regular regiments. This is usually exerted by the older members of the community who are active in supporting the army as a whole and the Territorial Army in particular. Many of them are members of the excellent Territorial Army associations and they do wonderful work. But their views are not always geared to the needs of the army, the geographic structure of the areas which the regiments are trying to represent many of which have changed out of all recognition in the last twenty years, or to the interests of those now serving, most of whom do not want to see their regiments broken up.

So far as the armoured corps is concerned in both the regular army and the Territorial Army, the system is similar to that of the one battalion infantry regiments, except that there is one four battalion regiment in the form of the Royal Tank Regiment (the individual units are in fact known as regiments rather than battalions) and the parent body, comparable to the division of infantry, is the armoured corps as a whole. In theory the system

148

is not ideal, because the units are too small to provide opportunities for moving people when it is in their interests to do so, but in practice individuals seem content to switch between regiments when necessary. It is also worth mentioning that the Cardwell regimental system never applied to the cavalry and the present system is the one which has existed from the start. Whenever there has been a need to reduce the number of armoured corps regiments the matter has been satisfactorily managed by amalgamation and the extraordinary contortions indulged in by the infantry have so far proved unnecessary.

From this short and admittedly superficial description of the regimental system it can be seen that it is, in its present form, economic in terms of overheads because they are almost entirely shared on the basis of the divisions of infantry and in the case of the armoured corps by the corps itself. But there are some disadvantages in terms of the flexibility of the regiments which only have one battalion, and there is a considerable difference in the standard of the battalions produced by the various regiments. Although it would be wrong to suggest that all the one battalion regiments produce less good battalions than the regiments which have two or three battalions, it is certainly more difficult for a one battalion regiment to achieve such good results. For both of these reasons there is a case for sorting out the regimental system, in so far as the infantry is concerned, in such a way that the advantages are retained whilst the anomalies are removed. It could be argued that the same factors affect the cavalry regiments in the armoured corps and that if the infantry regimental system needs sorting out, so does the cavalry system. Although this could be true, there are a lot of differences in the make up of the two 'arms' both in terms of the sort of people who join them, the rank structure of the units and the pattern of their postings, all of which means that the same system would not necessarily suit them both.

The next subject is weapons and equipment. It is often said that the best weapons are of little value unless they are manned by well trained men which is undoubtedly true. On the other hand the best trained men would get nowhere today if armed with

149

bows and arrows. The fact is that both men and weapons are important, but it is the weapons which govern tactics and this in turn determines how the men should be trained.

The biggest single equipment problem affecting the army's ability to carry out its commitments is that so much of the money available has to be spent on the troops in Germany in order to make them capable of taking part in highly specialized armoured and mechanized operations. If the army's main contribution to NATO was stationed anywhere other than in the Central Region, the equipment that they would need would be more compatible with their requirements outside the NATO area and for the defence of the United Kingdom. This is because outside the Central Region there is nowhere British troops are likely to be employed, which is suitable for the advance of tanks in mass. As a result a smaller proportion of the defending force would need to be equipped with main battle tanks and sophisticated armoured personnel carriers, whilst the remainder of the infantry could be transported in more lightly protected vehicles with a less impressive cross-country performance but armed with modern anti-tank missiles. There would also need to be an increase in the artillery component of the force, with particular reference to air defence artillery, and an increase in the number of helicopters.

It could be argued that eventually the same situation will prevail in the Central Region as a result of a decline in the effectiveness of the tank, but this is not the situation that prevails at the moment. Few issues generate so much heat as the future of the tank and as it is one that will greatly influence the future of land warfare it is worth looking briefly at it.

For many years short range missiles have been used against tanks, but they did little to challenge the tank's superiority. In the early 1970s longer range weapons started to appear which had a more radical effect on military tactics. Their first important test came during the opening stages of the war between Israel and the Arabs in 1973 when the Egyptians crossed the Suez Canal and used them to establish an anti-tank defence of their bridgehead. For a short time they managed to disrupt the Israeli attack, but the weapons were too crude to affect the outcome of the war. Since that time much more effective weapons have come into use and all NATO armies are well supplied with them. But the weapons still have some serious disadvantages, such as the fact that the operator must keep adjusting his aim for the whole time that the missile is in flight. This means that he has to be able to see the target for the whole of the period which may not be possible since it may become obscured. Furthermore the operator himself may not be able to survive if he remains exposed for such a long time. Other factors which are still acting in favour of the tank include the introduction of more effective armour and the fact that the warheads carried by missiles are of limited variety compared to those which a tank itself can fire.

But the march of science is moving against the tank and it is well within the limits of modern technology to produce a light weapon that can fire a missile which the firer can forget about as soon as he pulls the trigger. Furthermore it will also be possible to produce shells fired from guns, as opposed to missiles, with guidance systems capable of finding an individual tank and destroying it. Despite the improvement in tank armour, the probability is that in time the tank will cease to play such an important part on the battlefield as it has in the past fifty years. When that happens the tactical balance will swing firmly towards the defence unless new methods of conducting offensive action can be developed. Possible progress in that direction might result from a further development in the use of helicopter-borne forces but these would also be vulnerable to air defence weapons that are within the range of new technology.

It would in many ways be entirely helpful if future weapon developments acted in favour of the defence, since this would push the waging of war down to a lower and safer level in terms of escalation. But evolution of this sort lies in the future. For the moment it is only possible to base the requirements for weapons and equipment and the formulation of tactics on the situation that actually exists and this does not include a lot of weapons which are not yet in service. The real problem is to ensure that NATO develops the new weapons and brings them into service rather than the Russians and also that the NATO forces draw the right conclusions from them in time to alter their tactics and

151

organizations, thus being in a position to exploit them to the full. To do this it is important to look well ahead so as to expend as few resources as possible on the things that are phasing out and to use them instead to prepare for the future.

The history of war consists in large measure of examples of this not being done, to the grave discomfort of one side or the other. Sometimes these examples are of a sudden and unexpected disaster as when a vast number of French armoured knights were destroyed at Agincourt by a small number of half-starved English archers and men at arms. With hindsight it is easy to see how this happened and it is even surprising that the French were caught out in this way in view of the events of the previous fifty or sixty years. More frequently a country's mistakes have only become apparent over a longer period and, although some have proved fatal, some have been rectified in the nick of time. The failure of the Royal Navy to draw the right lessons from the development of submarines and aircraft, nearly proved disastrous to the British in the Second World War, because so much money was spent in the inter-war years on battleships, that there was not enough left for anti-submarine forces.

A military historian could doubtless produce hundreds of examples of these situations. If a thorough analysis was done, it would probably be found that many of the mistakes came about because the weapon, or equipment, or ship that became redundant, had acquired some aura or prestige that superseded its tactical significance and made it difficult to dispose of. Certainly that applied to the armoured knights of old, who could not easily be dispensed with because of the place which they held in the fabric of the country. It was also true in a different sense of the position which British battleships held in the national consciousness throughout the first forty years of this century. It is important that wrong decisions are not made about tanks for similar reasons. At present they tend to be seen as the ultimate symbol of military power and the yardstick by which a nation's military prestige is judged.

It can be seen therefore that the problem of ensuring that the army is correctly equipped to carry out its likely commitments is mainly one of shifting the emphasis away from the most expensive forms of armoured and mechanized warfare, in order to make up deficiencies in other directions, such as artillery, lightly protected vehicles to carry the infantry, extra helicopters, stocks of ammunition and stores suitable for use outside Europe, equipment to fit out extra signals and logistic units, etc. But this cannot be done until new weapons make it possible or until the British Army is moved from the Central Region. Whilst it remains there, it must be fully equipped to fulfil its role in accordance with the current tactical situation.

Before soldiers can be trained there has to be an understanding of the way in which they are going to fight in any particular type of war, e.g. general war, or limited war, or counter-insurgency. This is not designed to tie the hands of commanders in battle, since they must decide on what they want their men to do at the time, in the light of the prevailing circumstances and in accordance with the orders of their superior commander. Indeed, tactics merely means applying resources in accordance with prevailing circumstances in such a way as to achieve a specific tactical aim. But there has to be a basic doctrine on which men can be trained so that formations and units are turned out capable of reacting to the wishes of their commanders.

The chain of command of field army units at home and abroad, co-ordinated by the Ministry of Defence, is responsible for keeping this doctrine up to date, so that it takes account of the introduction of new weapons and equipment and of changes in the procedures of allies and potential enemies.

It is the responsibility of commanders throughout the field army to ensure that their formations and units are trained in accordance with this doctrine. The training of formations and units is known as collective training. It is the responsibility of commanders throughout the individual training organization to ensure that the individual officers and soldiers whom they are training to take their places in the field army are also trained in accordance with this doctrine. This type of training is known, somewhat naturally, as individual training.

Although the procedure for formulating doctrine and using it

153

as a basis for training is well understood and established there is a considerable mechanical problem which can make difficulties for commanders responsible for both collective and individual training. This arises from the fact that the process for formulating and disseminating doctrine takes too long, because the business involves putting forward suggestions that have to be agreed at various levels of command, and by allies, before they can be turned into training pamphlets, which in turn have to be printed and distributed throughout the army. Very often, therefore, commanders find that the advent of new weapons, or an organizational change, is obliging them to train along lines different to those outlined in the current doctrine. They then find that people joining them from an establishment in the individual training organization such as one of the Arms Schools or the Staff College, arrive with a different understanding of tactics to the one that they have recently worked out, because the new arrival has been trained in accordance with an approved doctrine that is out of date so far as they are concerned. This is a serious problem because of the influence it could have on the ability of formations to co-operate with allies and ultimately on the outcome of operations.

Although some progress could be made towards rectifying the situation by improving the technical arrangements for printing and disseminating new doctrine, the problem can only be solved by devising a much better method of formulating the doctrine in the first place which would cut out consultation with people outside the true chain of command such as the heads of the various 'arms'. Even if these people wanted to be objective, they have no direct access to the relevant data and can only formulate their opinions by discussing them with representatives of their own 'arms' within the chain of command which wastes time and invites the introduction of prejudice.

But establishing and disseminating doctrine is not the only problem concerning the training of the army. There are many others, most of which involve either the provision of resources or the establishment of priorities. So far as resources are concerned, the difficulty is partly financial because training is expensive in terms of the use of fuel, ammunition, the wear and tear on weapons and equipment and particularly in terms of the cost of manpower taken up to run the establishments of the individual training organization. It is also worth mentioning that there is no easier way of making short term savings in the defence budget than by curtailing collective training. This expedient is often resorted to despite the fact that nothing has such a disastrous effect as preventing units from carrying out the activities on which their usefulness depends and nothing is so illogical as to go to the expense of maintaining units that are incapable of fulfilling their function because they are inadequately trained.

Although no purpose would be served by going into this problem in great depth with regard to the general cost of training resources, there is one resource which is of such fundamental importance that it must be mentioned. That is land over which training is carried out. The provision of training areas faces the army with one of its greatest difficulties, and one that is not shared to anything like the same extent by the other two services for obvious reasons. But unless the army has access to sufficient land over which to train it might just as well not exist at all.

The army needs land of two sorts. It needs land where it can fire its weapons, known as ranges, and it needs land where it can practise tactics without using live ammunition. One of the problems is that, as weapons become more complicated their range increases and shells and missiles become more powerful, thus increasing the size of the danger area. Consequently new weapons cannot always be fired on old ranges unless the ranges are enlarged. Sometimes if the ranges are part of larger training areas where tactical exercises are designed to take place, the firing range can be extended without any new land being obtained but in this case tactical exercises are curtailed. Over the past twenty years more and more units which were formerly stationed abroad have been returned to the United Kingdom, thus increasing the requirement for ranges and tactical training areas. The past five years have also seen a steady increase in the size of the Territorial Army which needs access to ranges and training areas just as much as the regular army.

There are some factors which help with regard to the provision of training areas. The most important of these is the fact that

155

about one-third of the units of the field army are in Germany in peace and can be trained on land provided by the Germans. Each year some units based in the United Kingdom also train in Germany, Denmark or Norway for short periods which affords some further relief. Another mitigating factor is that some units travel to countries outside Europe, such as Canada, to carry out training for periods of up to six weeks at a time which not only relieves the training areas in the United Kingdom, but also provides experience of different terrain and climates. These overseas exercises are expensive in travel costs but they are of immense value.

But despite all of these palliatives there is still an acute and growing shortage of training areas in the United Kingdom and the amount of land owned, or leased, by the Ministry of Defence must be increased. Inevitably this would cost a lot of money, but that is not the main trouble. The real difficulty lies in the reluctance of politicians of all parties to raise the issue, because of the outcry that would undoubtedly be raised by various environmental groups and local associations. Although it is undoubtedly the duty of the politicians to disregard these objections for the sake of national security it would be electorally impracticable for them to do so unless the population as a whole can be brought to see the importance of the issue. It is a matter of getting people to realize that even more is required of them in the interests of defending their country than the paying of taxes. It requires a carefully prepared public relations exercise, mounted by the politicians with full military support, to get the people of Britain into the right frame of mind.

There are, of course, many other problems relating to the provision of resources for the training of the British Army but no other ones are worth singling out for inclusion here, as they are not directly concerned with rectifying the shortcomings in preparing the army for carrying out its commitments identified earlier. The only other point that does merit consideration is the priority given to the training for the different sorts of war with particular reference to the training of officers.

There is quite rightly a difference between establishing the priority given for preparing for the different sorts of war and the time spent training for them. The reason for this is that, although one sort of war may be given priority over another, the time that has to be devoted to training for it must also take account of the complexity of the subject. For example, even if preparation for counter-insurgency was given priority over preparation for armoured and mechanized warfare in Central Europe, it would still be necessary to spend more time training for the armoured and mechanized war because it is so much more complicated from the point of view of the units taking part. In practice this has little effect on the collective training of formations and units because they train very largely for the type of war relevant to their current role, e.g. the units in Germany spend all their time training for war in Germany unless they are under specific orders to prepare for a tour of duty in Northern Ireland. Where the dilemma does have to be faced is in the establishments of the individual training organization such as the Staff College.

At present there is little doubt that the priorities on which the individual training organization works are too heavily weighted towards the Central Region of NATO at the expense of all other commitments. This is only partly due to the complexity factor. Largely it is due to habit and the fact that changes in the circumstances which govern the sort of war that is likely to take place have not sunk into the consciousness of those responsible for formulating the training programmes. As a result too little emphasis is placed on counter-insurgency; peace-keeping is hardly taught at all; the forms of limited war likely to be encountered outside the NATO area are not considered in much depth, although the Falkland Islands war did stimulate a bit of interest in this field; and little thought is given to the operations which the army might become involved in within the United Kingdom itself, other than the defence of important installations.

But despite these reservations, which mostly concern tactical studies in the individual training organization and represent a minute part of all the training that is done, it is generally true to say that the standard of both collective and individual training in the British Army is very high: it is unlikely that any other army can compare with it in this respect. The British Army's success is due to the degree of latitude given to commanders in the way

157

in which they organize training and to the great professional skill of both the officers and non-commissioned officers who put it into execution on the ground. It is as well that this is so, since it enables units and smaller bodies of men to rise to the occasion in an emergency and produce a favourable result even if pedestrian direction further up the ladder leaves little opportunity for success. This situation is a great improvement on that prevailing in some armies where even the best laid plans are often bungled by the men on the ground.

Notes

1   The figures given in this paragraph relate to the situation as it was in 1985.

Chapter 10

OFFICERS AND MEN

In describing the army in Chapter 6 the point was made that in a very general sense the situation with regard to the recruitment and retention of other ranks in the full-time army was satisfactory, because a large number of the men and women who join in the first place leave after about three years, which ensures that the majority of those in the most exposed positions in war are young enough to survive the physical demands placed on them. At the same time enough stay to ensure that those promoted to the rank of corporal and above are adequately qualified by experience to fill the jobs which have to be done by non-commissioned officers. The other big advantage which is derived from this, is that because a high percentage of the men in the army are young, the number of men who are married is kept within manageable proportions.

But there are some grave disadvantages. The first of these is that many of the private soldiers leave just when they are becoming reasonably well trained and have to be replaced by new men with no military experience. The more specialized the role, the more necessary it is to have experienced men, even at the expense of having them a bit older. Furthermore the training is expensive. The second disadvantage is that the army plays no part in deciding which men stay and which men go: the selection is purely a matter of personal decision on the part of the men concerned. Often it is the more capable men who go, because they are the ones who find it easier to get jobs in civilian life. The third major disadvantage is that the system only works when unemployment is high. If the country moved into a period of full, or nearly full, employment it is doubtful whether enough recruits could be found to keep the army at its present strength, unless more of them stayed beyond their initial three years. Two ways of overcoming these disadvantages are often mentioned. The first is to bring back conscription and the second is to improve the conditions of service to the point where more men want to stay for longer.

Although conscription is impracticable, it is worth looking briefly at the arguments for and against it. In favour of the idea is the fact that it would ensure a steady flow of recruits, regardless of the state of the civilian employment market and of the conditions of service offered to the conscripts themselves. None the less, better conditions would still have to be offered to the regular component of the army which would be needed to train and lead the conscripts. Another argument in favour of conscription is that it would provide a greater number of trained Individual Reservists. A third advantage is sometimes seen as being the beneficial effect that a period of compulsory military service is supposed to have on young people and a fourth is the strengthening of the links which might grow up between the army and the civilian community as a result of it.

The disadvantages are first that it would be politically difficult for conscripts to be made to serve for longer than two years and, if the experience of continental countries is anything to go by, the period might be eighteen months or even less. In view of the complexity of the jobs carried out by most soldiers, relatively few could be successfully undertaken by men on such short engagements: in the British Army as it is today certainly no more than 45,000 of the jobs could be carried out by conscripts on a two-year engagement, probably less. But the number of able bodied men in the United Kingdom who reach the age of eighteen each year is getting on for half a million, so it would be difficult to devise a fair system for selecting the one-tenth that the army could use. Even if the rest were recruited into some form of youth service, there would be all sorts of arguments as to which boy would be selected for what activity and it is not even easy to see what the youth service could do, without putting other people out of work.

160

From an army point of view the disadvantages do not stop there, since there would be an increased commitment for recruit training as a result of the extra turn round of conscripts staying for eighteen months or two years as opposed to regulars staying for three years or longer. This would mean that more regulars would have to be diverted to the training of recruits and more resources in terms of buildings, fuel, ammunition and training areas would be needed to keep the army at the same strength. Although the conscripts could be paid very much less than the regulars they would be replacing, it is unlikely that all the extra cost of the training would be recovered, especially as the overall strength of the army would have to be increased to take account of the additional training commitment.

There are several other disadvantages to conscription bearing in mind the particular commitments that the British Army must be ready to fulfil. For example, the propaganda opportunities presented to an insurgent organization such as the Irish Republican Army would be increased if they could say that the soldiers opposing them were being forced into the struggle against their will. Furthermore, the greater the number of inexperienced men that there are in a unit, the greater is the chance that a mistake will be made in the handling of a tricky situation, which the insurgents could also turn to their advantage. Another disadvantage of a totally different sort is the danger that conscripts who have no desire to be in the army in the first place might spread discontent amongst the younger regular soldiers, thus increasing the likelihood of them leaving at the three-year point instead of staying for a further period.

In summary it can safely be said that the introduction of conscription would not be worthwhile, unless the full-time strength of the army had to be raised above the number that could be recruited as regulars without improving the terms of service to an unrealistic degree: indeed there may even be a limit to the number of people that could be persuaded to join the army voluntarily, regardless of the inducements offered. Although it is difficult to put a figure on the extent to which the strength of the army would have to be increased before conscription became a worthwhile option, and allowing for the fact that this figure

161

would vary according to such factors as the civilian labour market, there is no doubt that it will not be reached unless the international situation takes a significant turn for the worse. This could conceivably happen if a total ban on nuclear weapons was negotiated between Russia and America, as all NATO countries would have to make massive increases in their conventional forces as a result.

It is now time to look at the other option mentioned for recruiting and retaining the right men in the army, that is to say improving their terms of service which means their pay, accommodation and their way of life, together with that of their families. Naturally many of these improvements cost money which can only be found at the expense of some other defence requirement.

Most soldiers and even most of their wives understand that resources available for maintaining and improving their living conditions are limited and have to be balanced against other military requirements. In order to get them to stay in the army, however, it is essential that they should feel that their needs are being considered, that their views on what they would like are being sought, that such resources as are available are not being wasted and that they are being fairly distributed.

This is so elementary that it may seem surprising to find it even mentioned, but unfortunately the British Army, which has always prided itself on the way in which it caters for the needs of its men and women, does not always succeed in keeping abreast of developments in the country as a whole. One of the troubles is that the army made such great progress in the period immediately after the Second World War, that it has never got round to realizing that keeping abreast of events requires continual adjustment. Another difficulty stems from the fact that commanders are too apt to rely on their staffs to handle matters in this field and the staff branches which deal with them are seldom manned by the most mentally energetic and originally thinking officers, although they are usually highly conscientious and dedicated to the well-being of the soldiers.

Of the four requirements mentioned above, the most straightforward is ensuring that such resources as are available are not wasted, because this is merely a matter of efficient administration. But even the avoidance of waste is difficult because it hinges on a lot of people giving much attention to detail in a thoroughly unexciting area. It demands a high degree of personal interest by commanders throughout the chain of command. It also involves working closely with the many civilian organizations involved in the building and furnishing of quarters, the education of children, and so on, most of which are less efficient than the army at day to day administration.

When it comes to considering how available resources should be used to improve terms of service the problem is partly one of balancing the advantages of pay and pension increases against better living conditions in barracks and in married quarters. Another problem is concerned with the desire of married men to own their own houses against the time when they leave the army and this obliges the family to decide whether it is better to own their own house and face extra separation, or to live in an army house near the barracks.

There are many other matters where options exist for making use of available resources and the important thing is to know what it is that the men and their families want. If the aim is to keep the best men in the service, and if options exist for the use of resources, it is absurd not to know what the men and their families want, despite the fact that there are many factors which cannot be subject to their desires and which have to be taken into account before the decisions are made.

So far as service men and women are concerned, arrangements usually exist for discovering their views, providing that they are serving in units. These arrangements take the form of welfare meetings, etc. where views are deliberately sought at fixed intervals. The only danger is that in some units the meetings are badly run, or that they are not held sufficiently often. Furthermore, soldiers serving in small detachments do not always get properly canvassed.

It is far more difficult to get the views of the wives, because the main link between the army and the wife is the husband and in most cases husbands fail to keep their wives sufficiently well informed about what is going on. But there are other ways of keeping in touch with the views of the wives and various organizations exist such as the Families Welfare Service and the Federation of Army Wives Clubs which are very helpful in this respect. Each unit also has its own families officer. But unless commanders at every level take a continuous personal interest in the activities of these organizations communication rapidly becomes ineffective.

But no matter how carefully the views of the soldiers and their wives are canvassed and how efficiently and fairly the available resources are shared out, there are some factors which affect the satisfaction that a man and his wife get from the army way of life which cannot be adjusted to suit individual preferences. For example, there is the question of the extent to which the soldier feels that his unit is capable of doing its job. There is the amount of time that he is separated from his family which, in the 'arms', often runs at about six months in the year. There is the interval between unit moves when the whole family has to uproot itself and move elsewhere. Only the chain of command from the Chief of the Defence Staff downwards, can ensure that units are treated in such a way as to give the men and their wives a chance of leading good and useful lives.

In considering how to improve terms of service, it is worth remembering the one great asset which the army has and which it should certainly hold on to against all pressure. That is the fact that soldiering is a profession into which the individual becomes totally absorbed. There is no question of relating the amount of work he does over any particular period to his pay, which remains the same whether he is working for twenty-four hours a day on an operation or exercise, or whether he is working for short periods interspersed with sport and long weekends. There is no overtime and no undertime either for that matter. There are no restrictive practices, no union pressures to undermine a man's natural wish to give of his best, no shift working and no special contracts. The army gives a man an opportunity to combine with others in his own small circle, in pursuit of a useful purpose, for the benefit of the community as a whole. This is certainly one of its main attractions and one that is often mentioned by men who have rejoined after leaving and spending a period in civilian life.

164

In short, although current terms of service are adequate for maintaining the strength of the army in the existing state of the labour market, they are not sufficiently good to ensure that men stay for long enough for the best use to be made of their training and subsequent experience. A considerable improvement is needed which must be based, to some extent at least, on a more thorough analysis of what soldiers and their wives want. Although improvements in terms of service can be expensive, and although keeping men for longer would increase the number of married men in the army, with consequent additional expense, some of the money would be recovered because with a slower turnover fewer would need to be trained.

Manning the Territorial Army provides problems of a different sort. In general there is not much difficulty in getting recruits in the first place, but far too many leave during their first year, i.e. before they even complete their training. Although strenuous steps have been taken within the units to reduce the annual turnover, it still runs at around 30 per cent in many cases. Clearly it is impossible for a unit to reach a satisfactory state of training if so many of its members are changing round each year, especially as the training time available is far less than in the regular army. Considering the importance of the tasks that Territorial Army units would be faced with at the very start of a war it is totally unacceptable to adopt the line that nothing much can be done to improve a situation that some regard as being part of the nature of the Territorial Army.

Two things need to be done in order to sort out this weakness. First, more care should be taken to ensure that a potential recruit really is suited to the Territorial Army, which would involve discovering more about his background and his reason for wanting to join. Once in, every effort has to be made to keep in touch with the family of the man or woman concerned (there is a higher proportion of women in the Territorial Army than in the regular army) so as to retain their support for the sacrifice which they often have to make. Many units do very well in this respect, but not all.

The second thing that needs to be done is that much better financial inducements need to be paid to encourage men and women to stay in the Territorial Army. Obviously the basic rate of pay which a man receives when he is actually training is the main incentive in this respect, but equally obviously it is not enough on its own, since if it was the problem would not exist. The other incentive that is designed to persuade men to remain in the Territorial Army is the bounty they receive after being in for certain periods. These bounties should be paid on a far more generous scale and at more frequent intervals. The fundamental point that has to be appreciated is that despite the magnificent spirit which enables the Territorial Army to exist at all, people can only give up their time on a long term basis if they are adequately compensated. To do anything less is unfair on their dependants and the country should not ask too much of them. The army, and indeed the country as a whole, has taken the Territorial Army too much for granted. It will always be cheaper to cover a commitment by giving it to the Territorial Army rather than to the regular army, but if this is done the Territorial Army must at least be given the resources which it needs to do the job properly.

It can be seen that the system for recruiting and retaining regular soldiers is broadly speaking on the right lines, despite the need to improve terms of service to the extent that more of them remain in the army for longer periods. There are the right number of men of more or less the right ages and there is no waste caused by the necessity for employing them after their usefulness is finished. The same cannot be said of the officers.

In general the present system for recruiting, retaining and disposing of officers has been in force ever since the army reorganized itself after the end of the Second World War. Its essential features are as follows. Most of those wishing to become full-time officers, as opposed to becoming officers in the Territorial Army, join after leaving school or university and, if they are granted a regular commission and remain physically and professionally qualified, they can, with a few exceptions, continue in the army up to the age of fifty-five. These so called 'regular' officers are the people who hold most of the command and staff appointments in the rank of major and upwards. In addition there are a number of officers serving on short service commissions who usually stay for three years, although some extend their service for up to six or eight years. These people carry out many of the junior appointments within the units of the field army and within the training organization. There are various other groups, such as those who are commissioned from the ranks and those who hold special regular commissions which last for a set number of years; usually ten or fifteen. Many of these people hold administrative positions, but they are also used to supplement the other two groups within units or on the staff.

Whilst in outline the system has not changed much over the last forty years, a number of developments have taken place which have reduced its ability to provide the sort of officers that the army now needs. This is hardly surprising in view of the way in which warfare has evolved over the period; a period which is roughly equivalent in time to that which elapsed between the Boer War and the battle of Alamein.

These developments deserve examination. On the one hand tactics designed to take account of new weapons and equipment which involve intense round the clock fighting, can only be successfully undertaken by commanders and staff officers young enough and fit enough to withstand greater pressures than was formerly the case. On the other hand the obligation to provide regular officers with careers up to the age of fifty-five, has meant that what started as a relatively young officer corps at the end of the war has got gradually older as the years have gone by. Another important development has been what can best be described as rank inflation, that is to say jobs which were once carried out by an officer of a certain rank are now carried out by officers of one or two ranks higher.

There are three main reasons for rank inflation. The first is that for significant periods it was impossible to raise the pay of officers sufficiently to attract men of the right quality into the army: this happened whenever there was a government pay freeze and the easiest way round it was to increase the number of appointments which could be undertaken by men in a senior, and therefore better paid rank. The second was the desire to ensure that army officers doing a staff job, should be of the

167

equivalent rank to officers of the other services doing the same sort of job: Royal Naval officers were almost always a rank higher than their army counterparts. This pressure increased considerably with the establishment of the Ministry of Defence in 1964. A third cause of rank inflation was the steady reduction in the size of the army taken together with the need to go on providing opportunities for promoting people steadily until they reached retiring age: this meant that many jobs had to be upgraded in order to provide an adequate career structure. A good example of the result of this policy is that in 1956 when the army was between two and three times its present strength, it only had about one-third more generals than it has today.

Apart from rank inflation, two other developments have become more important as the years have passed. The first is that with the need to give officers a satisfying feeling of progression at a time when the army has been getting steadily smaller, it has become increasingly necessary to ensure that people move forward steadily in batches by age. If someone gets promoted too young, he holds a vacancy in that rank for a longer period, thereby denying it to someone else. Age has therefore become a key factor in promotion, independent of professional qualification. As a result officers have been taking key appointments at a steadily increasing age rather than at a younger age as should be the case if the battles of the future are to be correctly handled.

The second development is that as the years have passed and increasing numbers of ageing officers have had to be found employment, more staff jobs have had to be invented to cater for them: they would be too old to stay in units. But these men, although old, are for the most part competent and conscientious. As a result they have developed their jobs until they have become essential to the smooth running of the army as currently organized. So much is this the case, that units are sometimes left short of officers to ensure that the jobs are kept filled, even if it means that young men are taken to fill them. The only way in which this absurd situation can be reversed, would be to combine a reduction in the age to which officers are kept with a reorganization of the army which would greatly reduce the number of staff officers needed. This could easily be achieved by removing the secondary chain of command within the army and by incorporating the individual service departments in the Ministry of Defence into the Defence Staff.

Having done this it would then be necessary to restructure officers' careers entirely. With no obligation to keep people for longer than they are needed, it would be possible to promote officers as soon as they were ready for it, in terms of their ability and qualifications, without regard to their age; some would get promoted quickly, some with more experience and some at a relatively advanced age so long as they were not blocking the way for better men coming through.

Bearing in mind the sort of pressure that is likely to fall on officers in the various ranks, it would ultimately be desirable to have Commanders-in-Chief finishing their appointments after, say, five years in the job at about fifty. A rough indication of the age at which lower appointments would have to be filled by officers who were wanted for promotion up the ladder, can be worked out from the desirable age for Commanders-in-Chief, although there would be no reason why officers who were not wanted for promotion should not be appointed at an older age. On this basis the Field Army Commander in the United Kingdom and the Corps Commander in Germany would have to be into their posts between forty-three and forty-five: Divisional and District commanders would have to be appointed at around forty and Brigade commanders at about thirty-seven.

Only a few of the most senior appointments in the Ministry of Defence, such as the Chief of the Defence Staff, should be held by officers over fifty. Very senior staff appointments should be held by men of roughly the same age as the commanders of the same rank, but without any hard and fast rules being applied regarding age. Staff ranks should be kept down as far as possible, because senior staff officers invariably generate a pyramid of filters below them which constitutes a grievous waste of resources. Most of the useful work on the staff is done by majors. In the Ministry of Defence in particular, the rank for most of the jobs should be reduced and in all headquarters more use should be made of officers commissioned from the ranks or

169

of warrant officers to carry out the junior staff appointments since most of them are highly efficient administrators.

Clearly this situation could not be reached overnight: it could only be achieved over a period, by gradually reducing the age at which officers reach certain ranks and then ceasing to worry about age at all in terms of selection. The process would also involve changing the whole system of officer training so as to ensure that essential qualifying courses were carried out in time for the man to be ready for earlier promotion. It would also need to include a series of redundancy schemes with generous compensation in order to phase out the large number of officers now in the system in time with the reorganization which would make it possible to dispense with their services.

The reorganization of officer training would have to be geared to the needs of the new system. To take an extreme example, it would be no use sending people to the Royal College of Defence Studies for a year's course at the age of forty-five, as they would not have enough time left in the army to benefit from it afterwards. In practice the important thing would be to send those likely to reach the rank of lieutenant colonel on an improved and lengthened version of the Staff College course which would teach all the theory necessary to qualify them to command a unit or brigade, or to fill staff appointments on army or joint staffs. Obviously no course can do more than provide the theory. Most of what a man needs to know can only be got from the practical experience he gains as he goes along. It might be desirable to get a few people earmarked for promotion to major-general on a much shorter version of the course conducted by the Royal College of Defence Studies once they are brigadiers, but this is of very limited importance. There are many other courses run for officers to give them the specialist knowledge that they need to carry out particular functions, but most of these take place in the earlier stages of their careers and would not need to be greatly affected.

There are many other aspects to a reorganization of the officer career structure as radical as that recommended, two of which certainly deserve discussion. The first is the problem of making a shorter career than the present one sufficiently attractive, so that the right sort of boys are still prepared to join in the first place. The second, which is connected with it, is to consider what would happen to officers leaving the army in their forties, some of whom would have held highly responsible and influential positions.

It is best to look at the second of these problems first, since the prospect of employment after leaving is part of the inducement for joining. At one time there would have been no problem, because many appointments were available and well suited to senior officers when they left the army. Now it is more difficult because there are few colonies in need of governors and many civilian organizations such as the police who often took in retired army officers as Chief Constables, now prefer to employ their own people. On the other hand, under the new system, senior officers would become available for employment about ten years younger than they do at present which would give them a better chance to fit into politics, industry, business, the church and many other occupations. There is in fact every reason to suppose that a man wishing to make the army his career would be in a better position overall than he is at present. Relatively few officers now leave the army without trying to get another job and they often find difficulty in doing so because of their age. If they were five or ten years younger, their prospects would be better. The question of incentive to join is not therefore likely to suffer much once people realize and see in practice that a younger senior retired officer has good prospects.

The other part of the problem is to make sure that the army gives its officers a good career while they are in it. Under the system outlined, there would be fewer senior posts in terms of rank, but officers would get real responsibility in less exalted ranks and would not suffer the frustrations that dog them today once they leave their units and become enmeshed in the overstaffed organization that directs the army. But it is important to provide material incentives to match responsibility, which would mean increasing the pay of the lower ranks to take account of it. Thus, although the likelihood of reaching a certain rank would be less than it is today, the pay and pension of a lower rank, based on the responsibility that would go with it, would be just

171

as good and would be gained earlier. Providing these adjustments are made in a generous fashion, the attractiveness of an officer's career would be enhanced rather than diminished. Few people outside the army realize how galling are the frustrations of the present system to the able man: it is better suited to the mediocre which is why so many of the best officers leave when the end of their regimental service is in sight. If the army was officered in the way described it would not necessarily be much cheaper, because the need to increase the pay of each rank plus the need to pay pensions sooner, and therefore for longer, would offset some at least of the money saved by having fewer and less senior officers overall. The advantage would come from the fact that the army would be more efficient in peace and might even survive the additional pressures of modern war.

Before leaving the subject, it is only fair to point out one possible disadvantage which might well worry the politicians in peacetime. At present, in order to survive, all the senior staff officers in the Ministry of Defence and the senior commanders in the field have been obliged to develop a degree of conformity and understanding of other people's problems which makes them relatively easy to bargain with and manipulate. Furthermore, senior army officers are usually older and less energetic when it come to the in-fighting that goes on in Whitehall than the ministers with whom they have to deal. This state of affairs is achieved by holding up the rate of advancement of senior officers in the interests of providing balanced careers for all. It is done by diverting them periodically, into jobs outside the mainstream, where they pick up experience and lose time: they may even be given a year off altogether to go to a university or attend a mind-broadening course. Under the system advocated this would not happen: senior officers would be less tolerant, less experienced in the ways of the world, more energetic and more determined to get what they thought was necessary for the defence of the country. In other words it would be slightly less easy for the civil government to manage the army and retain its wholehearted support which is why the point has to be listed as a disadvantage. It would, however, be grossly overstating the case to suggest that the reduction of a few years in the age of senior officers would increase the likelihood of an army run *coup d'état*: there has never been the remotest possibility of this happening since the formation of the standing army in 1661.

It only remains to say that reorganizing the career structure of the officers of the army would be a difficult and painful business and the only justification for doing it is that it is essential. Experience shows that the piecemeal promotion of a few officers to senior rank at a slightly earlier age than usual has little effect: it is soon followed by a reversion to the status quo. Unless the reorganization is done thoroughly and enthusiastically the army will not be capable of carrying out its commitments in the future, despite the fact that its fighting units are without doubt the best in the world.

It is not without interest to see what happened during the Second World War. In 1939, the army consisted of excellent units indifferently directed from above by commanders and staff officers who were in many cases unsuited for the posts they held. As the war developed ages dropped and the ineffective were removed, so that after a few years the age factor ceased to operate for key individuals. Thus commanders of brigades could be found in their late twenties or thirties, commanders of divisions in their thirties and early forties and even the supreme allied commander in South East Asia was in his early forties. These young men worked perfectly well with older officers either as their superiors or as their inferiors. The problem in that war was that, as it progressed, the fighting qualities of some of the units dropped as a result of the vast influx of less well trained men sent to replace casualties, so that by 1945 the situation which had prevailed six years earlier was reversed. The direction had become highly effective whilst many of the units had become less so.

On the basis of this experience, it might be felt that there is no need to reform the existing system which works all right in peace, on the grounds that a better one would evolve over a period once a war started. But this overlooks the fact that there would be no time for this to happen in a world dominated by nuclear weapons. The peacetime army is the one with which a war would have to be fought and it must be capable of fighting well from the start.

The way in which officers are found for the Territorial Army is entirely separate and would not be affected by these reforms. The main reason for this is that there are very few Territorial Army officers employed outside units and so the age problem scarcely arises. The present system for selecting, recruiting and training officers for the Territorial Army has been greatly improved over recent years and further improvements are in hand. But these are no more than minor adjustments by comparison with the reforms recommended for the regular army and do not merit any detailed analysis in the context of this book.

Chapter 11

FINAL THOUGHTS

The time has now come to pick out some of the more important points made earlier in the book and to insert a few other relevant ideas which might otherwise have been omitted.

Achieving an understanding of the problems which face the army in carrying out its commitments is dependent, in the first instance, on realizing that warfare must be seen as a whole and that the various manifestations of it are but steps on the ladder of total war and interact upon each other. No one can understand the implications of waging war or the intricacies of doing so, unless they can comprehend the concept of 'warfare as a whole'.

The fundamental factor regarding war today is the existence of nuclear weapons. In the last resort they govern the level at which it manifests itself, and the way in which it is fought at each level. To some extent nuclear weapons serve the same purpose as Hell did before people ceased to believe in it, that is to say they have some deterrent effect on wanton acts of international wickedness. But they are also capable of reproducing in this world a situation not unlike the medieval concept of Hell itself when used.

As with Hell in days gone by, the threat of nuclear weapons is not totally effective at expunging evil from the international community. In practice what it achieves is to ensure that most war is waged at a lower level of intensity than would otherwise be the case. Without nuclear weapons as they are distributed today, the world would be a more dangerous place and defence would cost a great deal more than it does now, because nations would have to be prepared to wage war for much longer. The

175

aim of fighting major wars would no longer be to gain time for a ceasefire and would revert to breaking the enemy's will to fight. As described in the example given in Chapter 1, it would be necessary for the NATO alliance to have defences capable of holding the Russians for long enough for factories to be adapted to the war effort and for men to be called up, trained, equipped and sent to the battle. This would not only involve a vast expansion of the army but of the other services as well.

It is, however, essential to realize that the benefits which have been derived over the past forty years from the existence of nuclear weapons, have to some extent come from the way in which they have been distributed between the nations. Whether or not this distribution remains favourable to world peace in the future not only depends on the balance between Russia and the Western nations, but also on the way in which other countries develop their nuclear capabilities. The greater the number of nations that become nuclear powers, the more complicated will the business of preserving a balance become. The problem is how to control the balance rather than how to eliminate nuclear weapons altogether, because to eliminate them would be to forfeit the benefits which have accrued from their existence so far. The possession of really effective nuclear weapons by the United Kingdom not only enables her to be defended at less cost than would otherwise be the case, but also ensures that the country has some influence on negotiations concerning the way in which the nuclear balance is maintained in the future.

The deterrent effect of nuclear weapons depends not only on their destructive power, but also on the ability of the countries or alliances that own them to wage war at lower levels of operational intensity as well, so that minor outbursts of hostility can be prevented from escalating in a dangerous fashion. Only if these capabilities exist will rivalries involving nuclear powers be confined to the lower levels of warfare.

British arrangements for the provision of nuclear and non-nuclear forces reflect agreements made with allies at a time when the nuclear balance was different to what it is today, to say nothing of what it is likely to be in the foreseeable future. As a result of changes in the nuclear balance, some of the army's current commitments are not adequately covered. Furthermore, the commitment in the Central Region, which is adequately covered, is to some extent preventing the others from being handled effectively because of the nature of the task itself. It is impossible to make a sizeable contribution in the Central Region without being fully prepared for the most advanced forms of armoured and mechanized warfare both in terms of tactical doctrine, the training of officers and soldiers, and the development of weapons and equipment. This soaks up a high proportion of the resources available for defence as a whole. None of the army's commitments in other parts of the world or in the United Kingdom has the same effect.

The reason for the priority which has been given to the army's commitment in the Central Region has been as much concerned with reassuring the West Germans so that they remain within NATO as it has been with deterring the Russians, although the two functions are obviously closely linked. If a different role could be found for the British army such as the defence of Schleswig-Holstein, which was equally reassuring to the Germans but less heavily dependent on the most concentrated forms of armoured warfare, it would be more compatible with the army's other commitments. It would enable the army to carry out its commitments outside the NATO area and in the United Kingdom itself more efficiently and it would also make the army less vulnerable to the major upheaval which is bound to come when technology renders the tank obsolete.

With regard to the defence of the United Kingdom, the fact that the police have been enlarging their responsibilities in recent years needs to be understood, acknowledged and effectively funded. But even if this is done, the army must still be capable of fielding a larger force in the country in war than it now plans to do. Some of the extra can be made up of low grade infantry capable of doing no more than guarding installations or carrying out simple reconnaissance tasks.

When it comes to considering the arrangements which exist for directing Britain's defence effort as a whole and the activities of the British Army in particular, it is evident that there are shortcomings in both cases.

177

In the case of the higher management of defence the problem arises from the taking of two incompatible decisions. The first, taken after the Falklands war, was to make the Commanders-in-Chief directly responsible to the Chief of the Defence Staff for operational matters and the second, taken as part of the consequential reorganization of the Ministry of Defence, was to keep the individual service departments separate from the central Defence Staff. The first of these decisions was long overdue, met with little opposition and was completely necessary in terms of the efficient handling of defence. The second reduced the impact of the reorganization of the Ministry of Defence and was taken in order to stave off opposition to it and to avoid the political difficulties which would have arisen if it had included modifying the constitutional position of the heads of the three services. There is no doubt that the three service departments should be fully merged with the Defence Staff, not only on grounds of economy but also to ensure that there is no impediment to the free flow of ideas between the Commanders-in-Chief who have to implement defence policy and the Defence Staff which formulates it. The continued existence of the service departments constitutes, in effect, the establishment of a secondary chain of command, which can only complicate what is already a sufficiently complex business.

The army also is weakened by having its own dual chain of command which results in the direction above unit level being top heavy. It is important to do away with this and then to reduce the age of both commanders and staff officers. The first of these measures is needed in order to enable objective decisions to be made quickly in peace. The second is needed in order to ensure that the machinery for conducting operations can withstand the increased tempo of modern war. Apart from a natural reluctance to change an arrangement that has existed for many years, the main reason for the continued existence of the army's dual chain of command is that to abolish it now would weaken the hand of those in the Ministry of Defence who want to retain separate service departments within the Ministry of Defence. The two problems are therefore connected.

Another harmful side effect of using large numbers of staff

officers in the Ministry of Defence is that people with little genuine military understanding go on moving up through successive ranks purely on the basis of their administrative ability. As they get more senior they get given command appointments in the field army to widen their experience which they usually handle perfectly adequately, providing that no operations take place, by relying on ideas and procedures worked out by their predecessors and managed by their staffs. But most of these people are not really capable of exercising command which involves constantly adapting plans and procedures in the light of changing circumstances, to say nothing of making clear decisions and seeing that they are carried out regardless of difficulties if hostilities occur.

The effective exercise of command at every level is a most important factor in determining the success of operations and this applies as much to peace-keeping and low intensity operations as it does to those further up the scale. Naturally the machinery in Whitehall for funding, equipping and supplying the army must be right, together with the arrangements needed for ensuring that the government has a proper control over all defence activities. This is the sphere of high level administration, much of which should be carried out by politicians and civil servants, although there is also a role for some serving officers to ensure that the politicians and civil servants are fully aware of the needs and problems of commanders and their forces and to ensure that both parties understand each other. But no amount of skill on the part of these people will be of much use if the commanders in the field do not know their business. Increasing centralization in the 1970s drew into the Ministry of Defence a higher proportion of officers who would otherwise have held posts in the field army or individual training organization where they could have gained the experience needed to fit them for the command of forces on operations. Indeed in some cases field army formation headquarters had to be disbanded in order to produce the officers required to underwrite the needs of the Ministry of Defence, a process which has mercifully been reversed during the past six years.

A separate book could well be written on how an officer can

179

develop the skills and characteristics needed to exercise command, but for the present purposes it is enough to point out that he must spend most of his time gaining experience related to the waging of war in one form or another. The constant removal of high class officers to sit behind desks in London must have been partly to blame for the difficulty that the British Army has so often experienced in finding commanders capable of combining the efforts of many different arms in the face of the enemy. There is little doubt that the problem has been aggravated in recent years by the fact that the size of the regular officer corps has shrunk, as a result of which, although the number employed in the Ministry of Defence has not increased, the proportion has. Reducing the number of staff officers needed in the Ministry would go a long way towards ensuring that the army has an adequate supply of competent commanders.

A reduction in the age of senior officers, which would at least be possible if the number of staff appointments could be significantly reduced, would liven up the whole army in peace as well as war. It would result in fewer able officers leaving at the conclusion of their regimental service because the prospect of reaching highly responsible positions would be far closer and it would certainly ensure better opportunities for them in civilian life at the end of their military careers. More ex-senior officers would ultimately find themselves in influential positions in the civilian community from where they could promote the interests of the army and of defence in general.

The terms of service of warrant officers, non-commissioned officers and private soldiers need to be improved in order to increase the incentive for people to serve for longer than the initial three years. To be effective the improvements offered must so far as is possible be those actually wanted by service men and women and their families, which involves developing an efficient method for consulting them. Present arrangements for keeping in touch with the families are out of date and ineffective, especially when the serviceman concerned is serving outside a unit, e.g. in a large installation or headquarters.

Before concluding two points which have not so far been raised need examining. First, it could be argued that regardless of short term defence priorities, it would not be in the best interests of the army overall to weaken its commitment to the Central Region, because having one dominant commitment leads to a better allocation of resources and greater efficiency than having a number of lesser commitments each vying with each other. Brian Bond's admirable book on army policy between the wars would certainly indicate that this view is sometimes correct.[1] But the proposition only holds good if events develop in such a way that the master commitment remains so important that failure in other areas is unimportant by comparison with it. The shift that has taken place in the nuclear balance in recent years and the consequent change in the direction from which threats to the country's interests are likely to arise, indicate that some alteration in priorities is unavoidable.

The second proposition is that the savings which the army might make if it ceased to concentrate on armoured and mechanized warfare in the Central Region would not be used to make it more efficient elsewhere, but would be diverted to improving the position of the Royal Navy or the Royal Air Force. The answer to this is that if a truly objective examination undertaken by the Ministry of Defence showed that the defence of the country would be better served by diverting some resources from the army to the navy or air force it would be foolish not to do so. In the last resort the aim is to make the country secure rather than to promote the interests of the individual services. It is beyond the scope of this book to say whether this should happen, but the analysis given in Part 1 of the way in which a future war would be likely to develop gives little indication that the needs of either of the other two services should take precedence over the requirement for the army to put right the shortcomings described. But this is a matter for the Ministry of Defence and all that can be said here is that, since its recent reorganization, it is in a better position to produce objective assessments than it used to be: further adjustments along the lines recommended would increase its ability even more.

Finally it must be stressed that despite the forty years that have elapsed since the end of the last major conflict and notwithstanding the many suggestions made in this book for bringing the army up to date, there can be no doubt about the current high quality of its officers and men. The regimental system based on fostering a family feeling and imposing firm discipline, continues to enable the fighting units of the British Army to meet successfully the diverse challenges which confront them. At the higher levels the fact that some of the officers are too old does not mean that they are idle, incompetent or reactionary. Nor does the fact that some officers are employed on jobs which are not needed, or which run counter to the efficient management of the army, mean that they are bad officers. On the contrary they are often highly effective and it is not their fault if their best efforts are expended in ways which sometimes have a deleterious effect on the army in a wider context: they are only doing what they have been selected to do.

There is no doubt that Britain has an army of which it can be justly proud and this applies both to the regular and the Territorial Army. On the other hand unless its shortcomings are put right it is unlikely to meet with the success that it so richly deserves when a major challenge arises.

Notes

1   Brian Bond, *British Military Policy between the Two World Wars* Clarendon Press, 1980.

INDEX

183

184